LAST
GAMER
ST...ING

For all the girl gamers who've struggled to
find their place in the gaming world.
You belong, and you rock.

ONE

I am definitely going to die.

The darkness pressed in on me from all sides, blocking any possible escape routes. A sliver of sunlight peeked out through the thick canopy of Chinese elm trees surrounding me. Fireflies wove in and out of the leaves. The little creatures provided the only light illuminating who—or maybe *what*—I was fighting.

The WeiXian Forest hid both demon and human enemies alike. I'd taken down two nine-tailed foxes, or hú li jīng, and three human enemies using my trusty weapon: a red-and-gold-banded staff named the Ruyi Jingu Bang that could shrink or stretch to any size. In this forest, it wasn't uncommon to also run into è guǐ, or hungry ghosts, and guǐ pó, or demons disguised like old women.

At the moment, there were no demons nearby. Only two of us

were left. Once I took down the last enemy, I'd be home free.

Unfortunately, this last guy was good. I'd spent an hour exchanging blows with him, but we were pretty evenly matched. My Ruyi Jingu Bang alone wasn't enough to take down my opponent, so I'd been trying to construct a new weapon from the materials in my messenger bag. If I didn't make something powerful, and *quick*, I'd be in big trouble.

"All right, Proslayer," I hissed to myself. My breath fogged up the inside of my Codex, the VR helmet I always used in a match. I spun around in circles and held my weapon at the ready, the golden tip pointing into the dark forest. "Come out and face me, and let's end this."

The sound of wind rustling bushes answered me. At least, I hoped that was the wind, and not another hú li jīng or è guǐ waiting to pounce on me. The thrum of a steady rhythm in the distance grew faster and more frantic. Danger was near.

I clenched my teeth against the sudden chill. This showdown needed to end as quickly as possible. We'd been battling a little over an hour, and most matches were usually finished by now. While the suit softened the blow of in-game hits, my limbs were quaking from the exhaustion of combat. The sun had set, so it was getting harder to see through the thick growth of trees. I was running dangerously low on energy.

Something shiny on the ground caught my eye.

A bronze wire.

I snatched it up and placed it in my messenger bag. *Think, think, think.* I rummaged through the contents in there.

A wire—I could make something with that. A device to destroy the enemy. All I needed was a fuse and gunpowder.

I was *sure* I had those materials in here somewhere. My frustration grew as I continued digging through my bag, with no luck.

Then another glowing item emerged in a nearby bush. A peach. Energy. My avatar had taken on some damage, and I needed to restore my health bar. I reached down to pick it up, but before I could, a glint of silver slashed toward me from the left. I dodged in the nick of time and then sidestepped another flash from the right. Double swords.

Proslayer!

Finally, he was showing himself.

I ducked behind a giant elm tree. A flash of navy-blue armor disappeared behind a cluster of Chinese snowball bushes.

My target.

I reached into the contents of my bag to pull out some materials—wooden planks and a pickax. "A-ha!" I quickly piled the planks on top of each other, constructing a red-and-black pagoda-shaped house.

Not a moment too soon, either. Right as I disappeared into the protection of the house, Proslayer's sword slashed the spot where I'd been standing.

Ping!

That noise indicated a player had opened a new chat bubble. A message in neon-green lettering appeared in the left corner of my Codex's screen.

Proslayer: U gonna hide in there like a girl or are we gonna end this?

Fury spiked through me. Gamers like Proslayer liked to use "girl" as an insult in the most misogynistic way.

If there was one thing gaming had taught me, it was that nothing got on these players' nerves like returning their half-baked insults with smiley faces and proper grammar. They *hated* that.

I gritted my teeth. This was no time to let insults get the best of me. My gaming session, the first round of qualifiers for the Junior Dayhold Tournament, was currently being livestreamed on the Dayhold official eSports Live channel. Thousands of unnamed, faceless gamers and fans watched this final showdown between TheRuiNar and Proslayer from the comfort of their homes. They probably expected me to lose, since in last year's Junior Dayhold Tournament, Proslayer had not only qualified— he'd finished in the top ten. He was *really* good.

Of course, the last Junior Dayhold Tournament hadn't seen the likes of TheRuiNar. It was time to crank up my gaming and turn the tables on Proslayer. Nobody was getting between me and the grand prize.

Wire. Fuse. Gunpowder. Frantically, I sorted through tree leaves and flowers—the useless items in my bag. I vowed to organize the contents of what I'd collected as soon as this round concluded.

Time to get him tilted.

"Reply to chat with Proslayer," I commanded Codex.

TheRuiNar: I'm right here! Come and get me! :):):)

Proslayer: Get ready to cry for Mama, punk!!!

Proslayer's rage was practically palpable through the screen. I'm telling you, it was the smiley-face thing.

"Come to Papa," I growled under my breath. I didn't know if I was talking to Proslayer or to the items I was still frantically searching for. Probably both. I glanced at the screen on the right side of my helmet. My armor and health bars glowed an angry red. Practically empty. My virtual energy drained every time I took a hit, and I'd taken several already in this battle. I needed to replenish it—or else it was game over.

I could picture the peach from earlier still on the bush near Proslayer's boots, taunting me.

Seconds. I had seconds to destroy Proslayer—or he'd destroy me.

Then—*there*—the fuse and gunpowder showed up in my bag, side by side. I pulled them out and combined them with the bronze wire. The items glowed as they fused to form an explosive. Not a moment too soon.

Proslayer charged forward into the pagoda. He slashed with both swords toward me.

Unfortunately for Proslayer, I'd exited the house. I dove for the peach and devoured it in two chomps. Seconds later, my health level went up.

"Health level restored by fifty percent," said Codex's automated voice.

I ducked for cover behind a nearby cherry blossom tree and watched as the bomb I'd left in the pagoda exploded in a fiery burst of orange flames.

Who's crying for Mama now, punk?

Seconds later, a red message popped up in the space where the house had stood just moments ago.

PROSLAYER HAS BEEN ELIMINATED.

Then there was another *ping*, and a giant scoreboard replaced the previous message, red letters flashing bright. Next to each player's name and score stood their avatars.

THERUINAR: 89 points

PROSLAYER: 78 points

AMEFYST: 57 points

DUSTIN955: 49 points

RHCP: 44 points

ROUND ONE QUALIFIERS WINNER: **THERUINAR**

"Ha! Take that!" I punched my fists into the air. I did the body roll and then a dab, which was TheRuiNar's signature move for victory, inspired by one of my favorite K-pop idols, Yoomi.

I closed my eyes as the WeiXian Forest dissolved around me. The button on my gamer suit over my navel activated, and moments later, I was jolted back to reality—the holographic screen that connected me to the virtual reality world of Dayhold. I'd spent over an hour positioned within my gaming setup, and my aching muscles were definitely feeling it.

Taking off my Codex, I shook out my tangled hair and breathed in deeply. Adrenaline soared in my blood, and my heart hammered in my chest.

Another night, another gaming session down. Eighty-nine more points? Not too shabby! Points were only useful for the Dayhold store, where I could finally afford to upgrade my weapons and armor. This was the best feeling on the planet. The adrenaline rush of being in battle. The sense of accomplishment at outwitting an opponent in strategy.

The Junior Dayhold Tournament was only my second official tournament *ever*, and the tournament jitters had shaken me enough that I'd gotten off to a rocky start.

There was more at stake for me than the other players. As far as the Dayhold gaming community knew, TheRuiNar, like my avatar, was a teen boy. I had a very good reason for keeping as low a profile as I could.

Because the person *actually* behind TheRuiNar was a twelve-year-old girl.

TWO

Let's press pause and start over.

I was TheRuiNar. But I was also not.

In Dayhold, TheRuiNar was a male avatar with an awesome costume and hair (customized by yours truly). A rising star among the players.

Yet the person behind the screen was a short sixth grader with plain black hair named Reyna Cheng.

Or in Chinese, Rui Na Cheng.

I wasn't exactly *hiding* my identity. The other gamers just assumed that my avatar reflected my real-life self. When people did ask me for my Dayhold username in real life, I had a whole alt account prepared, of course: ReyningChamp (which was a pretty clever name, especially for a fake account, if I do say so myself).

Having my main account feature a female avatar in the Dayhold world would be an invitation for trash talk from the male gamers, a lesson I'd learned the hard way.

Four years ago, when I first started playing Dayhold, I'd created a female avatar and named myself Pandagrlrox. But every time I joined a practice battle, the guys would mock my gameplay for being "too girly," whatever *that* was supposed to mean. After a year of constant teasing, I decided to scrap my first avatar and come up with a new one. Hence, TheRuiNar was born. Someone who looked and acted tough. Someone the male gamers would accept into the Dayhold community.

Gaming was dominated by guys, so it wasn't a surprise that Dayhold Academy was a total boys' club, too. There were four hundred students enrolled, some of them full-time students and some of them only enrolled for the 2067 summer camp. Just seventy-eight of us identified as girls. The pro Dayhold teams, like Fuzion, scouted from Dayhold Academy. That meant that there was fierce competition among students. And since plenty of students were participating in the Junior Dayhold Tournament this summer— some publicly, some not so publicly—tensions ran higher than ever.

The sound of footsteps in the hall jolted me out of my post-livestream euphoria. I checked the digital clock on my nightstand. It was already a quarter to ten, which meant lights-out was in fifteen minutes. The caretaker, Mr. Porter, was making his rounds through the dorm halls, checking that we were all ready for sleep.

As I was about to turn in for the night, my xPhone 7 vibrated on the bed. *Baba,* flashed the caller ID on the screen.

I glanced at the door, listening as the sound of footsteps moved past my room and then down the hall. A quick call wouldn't break the rules.

"Hi, Baba," I whispered. The xPhone 7 was one of the older models of the xPhone but still possessed advanced functions, like being able to pick up my voice from across the room, so I could talk as quietly as I wanted.

"Rui Na." Rather than sounding warm, my father's voice carried an edge of panic. "I wasn't sure if you were still up."

I suppressed a yawn and said sleepily, "I'm about to go to bed."

"I wouldn't normally call you so close to curfew, but this is an emergency. Your mother is in the hospital again."

A lump formed in my throat as reality came rushing back to me like a tidal wave. Now I was wide awake, my father's words reminding me of the ugly truth. Mama was sick with cancer. She had been for a few years now. "Again? I thought Mama just got back. Is she okay?"

"She will be okay. When are you coming home to visit, though? Your mother misses you."

I translated Baba-speak in my head: *We both miss you.* Not that my stoic Chinese father would ever admit anything as mushy and emotional as *missing* me.

My parents had fretted over me leaving home—Brooklyn—for summer camp in the heart of Manhattan. Even though camp was only a half-hour train ride from home, Baba and Mama were so protective of me, their only daughter. They had always been.

"I . . . I can't come home until after the camp is over, remember?" I reminded my father, guilt suddenly twisting my gut. "That's in late August."

Home. I missed it dearly. I pictured my family's small brownstone apartment. The stack of medical bills on the kitchen counter from Mama's hospital trips. The cabinets stuffed full of her pills and medicine. The guilt surged again, along with fresh motivation.

My parents had agreed to let me attend Dayhold Academy's

summer camp because six months ago I'd participated in the Spring Dayhold Games. It was TheRuiNar's first appearance in an amateur tournament—and I'd surprised everyone, including myself, by taking home third place. It was a big deal for a no-name gamer. Commander Dayhold, founder of the game and president of the academy, reached out to me personally to offer a scholarship to attend the academy and encourage me to enter the Junior Dayhold Tournament.

It was the chance of a lifetime—a chance that I never thought I'd get. After a lot of begging, I convinced my parents to let me enroll. They just didn't know I wasn't exactly playing as myself. Most professional Dayhold players were male, and there were so few well-known pro female gamers that I could name them all off the top of my head. M00nshine. LuckyJade847. LuckyTrix. AvengingAngel.

Right at the start of camp, a message went out to the whole school:

FUZION PRESENTS:
THE JUNIOR DAYHOLD TOURNAMENT
(Ages 13 & Up)

A Battle Royale to End Them All!

Qualifiers: Monday, August 8 to Sunday, August 14

Tournament: Monday, August 22 to Sunday, August 28

GRAND PRIZE: $10,000 and meet & greet
with the Fuzion team

RUNNER-UP: $3,000

Rules: Players who would like to take part in the Junior Dayhold Tournament will need to finish with enough qualifying points to be among the top 100 by the end of the qualifying week.

Ten thousand dollars. The contest hosts were offering the winner *ten thousand* dollars. Everybody couldn't stop talking about the tournament. With that kind of money, Baba could pay off Mama's medical bills—and more. We could get her the best treatment in the world for her stage two breast cancer. There were only three of us in my tiny family. Like always, I had to do whatever I could to keep our family glued together. And maybe there'd be money left over for nicer meals, not just spaghetti with tomato sauce and hot dog chunks. Maybe there would even be money left over for all of us to finally take that trip to China we'd been talking about for ages but couldn't afford. Travel by electric-powered bullet airplanes—the most advanced transportation of today—was way out of our price range. It would be my first time seeing China, ever.

Plus, the winner would get the chance to meet and *play* with the Fuzion team. They were only one of the top pro e-sports teams in the world. The members were, like, gods in the Dayhold world. LuckyJade847 and M00nshine were also on the Fuzion team. Their posters decorated my dorm room at Dayhold Academy. Getting to play with my heroes was a prize beyond my wildest dreams.

If I won the Junior Dayhold Tournament, my parents would finally understand my dream of being a pro gamer. To me, Dayhold was so much more than just a game. Video games gave me a sense of accomplishment that I didn't get at school or anywhere else. I mean, there was no better feeling than defeating a demon.

It was a whole new world to escape to when the real world wasn't looking so hot. Like when Ye Ye, my grandfather, died three years ago. Baba, who never cried, *ever*, sobbed for days, and I didn't know what to do except watch helplessly. Or now, with Baba struggling to pay Mama's medical bills with his engineering job at Dayhold and Mama slowly losing energy every day. On days when

I felt down, I escaped into a fantastical world where I could be in control—mostly. I still had to keep my true identity a secret.

"Good night, Rui Na." Baba had been so silent on the other end of the phone that I thought he'd fallen asleep.

"Good night, Baba."

The next day in class, all anybody wanted to talk about was the previous night's qualifiers. Our professors set aside some lesson time to discuss the results and the competitors' gameplay.

Dayhold Academy was split into two age groups: silver level, students ages eight through twelve; and gold level, students ages thirteen through seventeen. Only the gold-level students were old enough to qualify for and compete in the Junior Dayhold Tournament. Since I was the sole scholarship recruit from the silver level, though, Commander Dayhold had made an exception for me.

It worked out in my favor. Nobody would ever suspect that twelve-year-old newcomer Reyna Cheng had qualified for the tournament, which meant I was free to keep my true gaming identity under wraps. There was pretty much no danger of me being doxed. But it did mean that I would have to play and practice twice as much as my classmates, as both TheRuiNar and ReyningChamp.

Hardly any of my silver-level classmates paid attention to our morning lectures. In Professor Lucien's Intermediate Strategy course, we were supposed to be silent-reading the next chapter in our *Dayhold Battle Strategies* textbook, which was all about feigning tactics. But the professor had to keep shushing students for whispering behind their books. A similar pattern followed in Professor Nelson's History of Virtual Reality.

"Are you all even going to bother *pretending* to pay attention?" shouted short, squat Professor Nelson after trying and failing to interest the class in the achingly boring stages of development of Codex.

In his Gaming Nutrition class, Professor Nakamura gave up entirely and spent his lesson discussing the qualifying-round results with us. I flushed when he wrote "TheRuiNar" in big block letters using the stylus on the holographic board. It was on a list with a few other usernames of the players whose gameplay had impressed him the most.

The conversations continued after class, too.

"Did you see TheRuiNar play last night?" Liam Russ was asking

Sanjeet Singh as I passed by them on the way to lunch. I almost tripped over my own shoelaces. They both gave me funny looks before turning away.

Sanjeet said, "Yeah, dude has some sick moves. Swear he came out of nowhere, too."

"Right? TheRuiNar totally blasted Proslayer. Took him out with an explosive right when he was about to run out of energy."

My cheeks prickled with heat. I couldn't help it when I heard my username mentioned like that. I wished I could have turned around to thank Liam for the compliment.

"And Proslayer is, like, a *ranked* player from previous tournaments. This new guy is pretty much a nobody!" Liam continued.

A nobody? I take that back. No thanks for you, Liam.

"Not a nobody. TheRuiNar won third place in the Spring Dayhold Games," Sanjeet pointed out.

"Yeah, but that was just one time. Could've been a fluke." Liam waved his hand through the air.

Someone tapped me on the shoulder. Well, I say tapped, but it was closer to *smacked*. "Hey, Reyna, what'd you think of the round-one qualifiers yesterday?"

I turned around to face Henry Amano, or HeyAmano, which he

went by in the Dayhold universe. My best friend's brown eyes shone with curiosity. I imagined telling Henry the truth. ("It was great. I was playing as TheRuiNar, and I smoked Proslayer. Surprise!") As hilarious as it would be to see the reaction on his face, there was no way I could admit to that, even to my best friend. Henry had the biggest blabbermouth of anyone I knew.

"Those qualifiers were definitely . . . something. Strong competitors last night, huh?" I said.

"Tell me about it. Did you see TheRuiNar? Everyone's talking about him today. He took out *Proslayer.* Guess TheRuiNar's impressive showing at the Spring Dayhold Games was for real!"

I cleared my throat and tried to appear as nonchalant as possible. "Yeah, TheRuiNar seems pretty awesome." Hey, I *was* proud of the victory I'd pulled off last night, especially given that it had been only my second amateur e-sports battle in public.

Henry stroked his chin. He kept doing it for the longest time, as though he were deep in thought. "Henry, you don't have a beard. You don't even have stubble," I reminded him.

"TheRuiNar versus F3lx," Henry said at last, ignoring me. "Now that'd be the *ultimate* matchup. I wonder who'd win in that showdown."

Just the mention of the username F3lx was enough to put me in a foul mood. F3lx was a livestreamer and one of the top junior Dayhold players around, but only because he wasn't afraid to fight dirty. F3lx also happened to be a gold-level student at Dayhold Academy. The popular, blond-haired, green-eyed Felix Matthews, a poster child for e-sports everywhere.

I never wanted to play against F3lx. Not because I didn't think I could beat him, but because I didn't want to put up with any of his dirty fighting. Hopefully someone else would take him out of this tournament before we ended up facing each other.

"TheRuiNar would win against F3lx, of course," I sniffed.

Henry frowned and cocked his head to the side. "You sure about that? I think I'd put my bet on F3lx."

"Mmmm."

Even though I didn't vocalize my thoughts, Henry could tell what I was thinking, because he said defensively, "Okay, so maybe the dude doesn't have the cleanest reputation, but you gotta admit he's still got some pretty solid moves."

The bell rang, signaling that it was time for lunch. I just shook my head, heaved an exaggerated sigh of disappointment, and walked away without another word.

"What? Was it something I said?" Henry called after me.

In the cafeteria, I slid into my usual spot at an empty table in the corner. Call me antisocial, but I didn't see the point in making friends, since everyone around me was competition. Also, being one of the few girls was pretty intimidating and made it even harder for me to summon the courage to try to make friends. Why would I want to be friends with a bunch of stinky guys who had burping contests during lunchtime? No thanks.

I watched Mimi Huang walk up to a holographic screen at the back of the cafeteria to order. Moments later, a cheeseburger with fries came down a chute and landed on a tray in the pickup area a few feet away. Mimi walked her tray over to the drink dispenser and pressed another button on the holographic screen beside it, and a bottle of orange juice came out of the dispenser, landing neatly on her tray. Dayhold's state-of-the-art technology meant no more crabby old lunch ladies, but unfortunately the food here was the same as any school cafeteria's, which meant we had to eat cardboard-like pizza and questionable hot dogs for days.

I preferred to eat alone, but after a few minutes, Mimi, Sanjeet, and Liam sat down in the empty seats at my table, carrying their trays of food. Mimi's gamertag was Meemers. Sanjeet went by SuperSaiyan8. And Liam played under BattleBoss.

I'd brought my own food today—a pack of green-tea-flavored sunflower seeds and some dried seaweed—which my parents had given me before I'd left for camp. It wasn't much, but my favorite snacks reminded me of home and temporarily cured me of any loneliness.

Luckily for the Junior Dayhold Tournament hopefuls, we got *great* in-room snacks, like chips and sodas, before our games, thanks to Fuzion's generous sponsorship. I definitely planned to take advantage of them before the next round tonight.

"I can't believe how intense the qualifiers were last night," whined Mimi, who sat in the chair next to me. She tugged at her pigtails. "I know there's a lot of cash involved, but it was only the first round. And this tournament is supposed to be just for fun, anyway. Jeez!"

"It's not 'just for fun' when there is ten thousand dollars on the line," Sanjeet informed Mimi with a serious expression. "That's a lot of money. That's, like, a lifetime supply of cheese!"

"Who the heck wants a lifetime supply of cheese?" Mimi said, gagging. "I guess you're right, though. That's a ton of money, and—" Her eyes widened, and she gasped, dropping the rest of the cheeseburger onto her plate.

Mimi's gasp was echoed by gasps and cheers around the cafeteria. I looked up and immediately located the source of all the noise: Felix Matthews. F3lx. Wearing a gray hoodie and black jeans, he strode into the cafeteria with a few of his popular gold-level friends, all guys. He raised a hand to acknowledge the students who were fawning over him. Cool and collected, as always.

I rolled my eyes. Everyone at school treated F3lx like a celebrity. I mean, I guess he kind of was one since he was one of the most popular Dayhold livestreamers. But he wasn't the *only* good player around. And I'd prove that to the school—and the Dayhold world—during this tournament.

"There he is, the man of the hour," Liam said, with a sigh full of admiration. "One day I'm gonna be as good as F3lx." He puffed out his chest and glanced at Mimi.

"Yeah, keep dreaming, Liam," Mimi snorted. Liam looked happy instead of offended, though. I think he was just content his crush was talking to him. Go figure.

"You don't wanna be like F3lx," Sanjeet warned. He cast an anxious gaze around the cafeteria. F3lx had that effect on Dayhold gamers. Some were scared of the guy, like he was everywhere, all the time. "He's pretty much indestructible."

"Yeah, and isn't that a good thing?" Liam said.

Sanjeet shook his head. "Nah. It's suspicious, is what it is. Bet you anything F3lx is getting some extra . . . *help*."

"Those are just rumors," Liam protested. "I mean, people accused him of cheating, but nobody could find any evidence."

Sanjeet went on as though Liam hadn't spoken. "If you're gonna aim to be like someone, you wanna be like TheRuiNar. Came out of nowhere and owned a ranked player in the tournament's first round. *Incredible*. Man, I love a good underdog story." He smiled in satisfaction, as if he were the one who'd defeated Proslayer.

There was my username again. I stiffened. Even though I knew there was no way my classmates would guess my Dayhold identity, I couldn't help but feel nervous at the thought. I'd hid my true identity for so long.

I did my best not to draw attention to myself, but unfortunately eating sunflower seeds quietly was not one of my strong suits. I swear the sound of my teeth biting against the shells could be heard within a fifty-mile radius.

"Reyna, what did you think of the qualifiers?" Mimi asked, blinking at me, as though the noise had just made her realize I was still sitting here.

I jolted. "Oh, um . . . it was cool," I mumbled. Silence. They clearly expected me to elaborate, but I clammed up. After an awkward silence, Mimi, Sanjeet, and Liam continued their conversation without me.

The rest of the school day passed in a blur. Round two of qualifiers for the Junior Dayhold Tournament was scheduled for later in the evening, and that was all I could think about. Only the top one hundred players would make it into the tournament, and thanks to last night's win over Proslayer, I only needed to win this second qualifier.

As soon as I got to my room, I ordered a hamburger, Caesar salad, and vanilla milkshake from the holographic screen. The food materialized in the food slot off to the left of the screen. It was my first square meal of the day, and my mouth watered at the delicious smell. I eagerly dug in, too hungry to care about how messily I was eating. Nobody was here to see me, anyway.

After I'd finished my dinner, I still had an hour to kill before the start of qualifiers. I put on my Codex and calibrated it to the holographic screen, and then I was through to my Dayhold player files. *WELCOME, THERUINAR* flashed in big, bold white lettering in the middle of the screen. On the left side, there were a few different icons: an envelope for my email, a document for the Dayhold rule book, and a round gold coin for the Dayhold shop. I had earned 89 points total so far. Doing poorly in any of the three qualifying rounds didn't necessarily mean being eliminated from the Junior Dayhold Tournament, but it did mean losing out on earning these crucial points, which could be exchanged for new armor, a weapons upgrade, or special items that would come in handy during the tournament.

I browsed the digital shop for a bit, taking my time to carefully select what to spend my precious coins on. The logical part of my brain knew that I'd earn more the longer I was in the tournament, but another part of my brain—I'd been raised by frugal immigrant parents, after all—cringed at the idea of splurging on too many shiny new things. Like a hot-pink sword. Okay, so it was shiny and pretty, but who needed a hot-pink sword when it cost two hundred coins?

Weapons were important, which was why they were so pricey, but I didn't see the point in overloading on them. As long as I had one really good weapon that I could continue to upgrade, I'd be able to advance rapidly through the rounds. It wasn't like I could wield more than one weapon at a time in battle.

The Ruyi Jingu Bang was the staff I'd chosen from the starter menu, out of many options. It was a legendary weapon from Chinese mythology, one of the most powerful of all. It was also the same weapon that LuckyJade847 used when she played in pro tournaments. Using the red-and-gold-banded staff made me feel one step closer to my idol. Also, it was just a freaking *cool* weapon.

I finally settled on buying more healing peaches. They were cheap and handy in battle. I also upgraded my staff so that it was longer, which would aid me in taking out opponents more quickly. Since I'd used up some items in the last round, I also picked up new copper wires and fuses. And finally, I snagged a cloak, which would essentially allow me to turn invisible—sort of. Opponents could still see me, but they wouldn't be able to see my heat source register in their helmets, which made the cloak the perfect weapon for sneak attacks.

My Dayhold wallet considerably lighter, I exited the shop and took off my Codex. Only thirty minutes left until the second round.

It was time for my pregame ritual, which was sort of like my good luck charm. Picking up my xPhone, I scrolled through my playlists and blasted the one titled "K-pop faves." Immediately, a BXS song began blaring out of the phone speakers.

Dancing to the beat and attempting a body roll in real life—it did *not* go as well as it did in virtual reality—I opened up my closet. An array of stylish gamer suits in every color of the rainbow greeted me. The gamer suits were necessary for VR play in the world of Dayhold. After a few minutes' debate—selecting the right outfit was important, since I didn't want to look like a total scrub—I chose a purple gamer suit. The BXS song changed to a song by Once, my favorite K-pop girl group. Dancing off beat, I reached over to my dresser to pick up my Codex.

Placing the headset over my head, I stood in front of the holographic screen. I reached out a finger to boot up my system and log in to Dayhold. The system took a few moments to sense my helmet and calibrate it to the Cloud, the data storage center that linked up players' gaming suit data with the virtual reality world. Once the calibration was done, the screen glowed.

Another evening, another round of qualifiers. Now that classes were over for the day, I could begin my *real* work.

I pressed the button on my Codex's right side and the real world and all its problems disappeared around me as the virtual world of Dayhold unfolded before my eyes. The setting for this game was different from the last round. The Great Wall of China stretched out before me, the stones weathered and real looking. I reached out to touch it, and it felt rock solid beneath my fingertips.

Already, I spotted a nine-tailed fox with red eyes charging down the steps toward me. Above it, *50 Points* hovered in red lettering. I drew my Ruyi Jingu Bang out of my messenger bag. It was time to defeat some creatures and gamers and rack up even more points.

Don't worry, Baba and Mama. I'm going to win this tournament for our family.

THREE

After I had made it through the second round, comments from onlookers flooded the livestream. Viewers couldn't see players' in-game chats and players couldn't see the livestream's comments until they were out of the game.

Normally, I avoided peeking at the comments after finishing, but this time I didn't resist the urge. I regretted that choice almost immediately.

Anon12: Good job, bro!!!

Anon2: THERUINAR GONNA KILL IT MAN

Anon23: dude this tournament is gonna be so dope hope u win my guy!!

It wasn't just cheers, though. The insults came, too.

Anon38: dude u fight so girly lol nxt time just finish the other guy in one blow

Anon49: looks like this noob had some good luck, but it's gonna run out in r3

I was unfortunately used to seeing these kinds of messages in the Dayhold community, but there weren't that many, thankfully. It wasn't nearly as bad as the bullying that gamers like LuckyJade847 and M00nshine faced on the regular in the pro Dayhold circuit. Guys telling them that their wins were flukes and that they belonged in the kitchen and not on the Dayhold battlefield. Some even threatened to find out where they lived. The thought of angry strangers tracking down their homes and families was terrifying. If they could do that, they could easily find out where *my* family lived. Anonymous gamers felt like they could say and do anything they wanted without facing any consequences, just because nobody could see their faces behind the screen.

That was the reason why I avoided using certain aspects of the game, like voice chat. If these Dayhold gamers heard a female voice, they'd be ruthless with the bullying. Thankfully, the tournament rules forbid voice chat for safety reasons, but even during a regular match, where it was allowed, I never used it.

Six months ago, LuckyJade847 took a monthlong hiatus from playing Dayhold because the cyberbullying got so bad. Seriously, who needed *that*?

I wished more than anything that I could retort, "I *am* a girl, thank you." But I wasn't as brave as LuckyJade847 or M00nshine. I just wanted to play Dayhold in peace—or as much peace as I could get in a battle royale game. I imagined the gamers fist-bumping each other after each insult and then going off and cracking "gamer girl" jokes for the rest of the day. Yeah, some of the guys who played Dayhold were just great.

Anyway, there was no time to think about sexist gamers. Right now, I had to focus on the qualifiers—and after that, the tournament itself.

The tournament would start with a player-versus-player elimination round, with one hundred participants who'd be competing at first, until half that number remained. Round two would take fifty down to twenty-five. Round three was different—a team elimination round that would take twenty-five down to just five in the last round. There, they'd battle until only one was left and crowned the winner.

"... Reyna? Earth to Reyna!"

I jolted out of my reverie and turned to stare at Henry, who was waving a hand in my face and giving me a concerned look. I shook my head. Right. I was at school, in the middle of Professor Kumar's Dayhold Geography class. "What do you want?"

"New kid," Henry said, pointing toward the front of the room. "He looks like a *serious* fanboy."

I glanced up. An Asian boy I'd never seen before in my life stood at the front of the class. While I'd been daydreaming ways to cream the competition in the Junior Dayhold Tournament, the professor had been introducing our new classmate.

The new kid clearly had no interest in hiding his ... *passion* ... for Dayhold. He wore a navy-blue Dayhold T-shirt and a black backpack that looked just like the ones in the game. Black sunglasses sat on top of his hair, which had red highlights. Something about his outfit struck me as oddly familiar.

"The new kid's got the same hairstyle as TheRuiNar's custom avi," Henry whispered. It sounded like he was in awe. I couldn't blame him. I mean, I was kind of in awe, too.

My jaw dropped. Henry was right. The new kid's outfit seemed familiar because it looked like TheRuiNar's, down to the black sunglasses.

"Class, this is Nell Kwon," said Professor Kumar. "He's a late addition to the academy, so I'll ask you all to help me catch him up to speed. Nell, please introduce yourself to your new classmates."

Nell gave us a huge, toothy grin. He must've been the only kid in the history of ever who was actually excited about the idea of introducing himself to a whole classroom full of strangers. What a weirdo.

"I'm Nell. I'm from Sacramento, California. I was born on November 24—"

"Jeez, this guy has a whole speech memorized," Henry muttered. Others in the class seemed confused by the amount of information Nell was sharing, and a couple of the girls started giggling in the corner. If Nell noticed, he didn't seem to mind or care.

I watched Nell with curiosity. I couldn't quite put my finger on it, but something about the new boy and his eagerness was just . . . intriguing to me.

Nell beamed at us as he continued regurgitating his whole life's story. As he spoke, he gestured with his hands. A lot. "My hobbies include playing Dayhold, watching livestreams of Dayhold, buying Dayhold merch—and oh yeah!" He snapped his fingers. "I've got my eye on this *awesome* new Dayhold player called TheRuiNar."

I stiffened and then quickly tried to relax.

Nell continued, "I'm planning to design some merch for him, so if anyone wants to chip in and help—"

"That's great, Nell!" interrupted the professor. He clapped his hands together. I joined in with the smattering of applause. "Splendid introduction."

Nell puffed out his chest. "Thank you, sir. I wrote it on the airplane—"

"Unfortunately, as I do have to start today's lesson, we will have to hear the rest another time," Professor Kumar said apologetically. He pointed toward an empty desk in the back of the classroom. "That's your seat over there. Welcome to Dayhold Academy."

Twenty pairs of eyes followed Nell as he practically skipped down the row toward his new seat. As he passed by me, his eyes met mine. I quickly looked away, my heart hammering in my chest. Even though I knew it wasn't possible, for a moment I'd been terrified that Nell's sharp eyes would recognize me as TheRuiNar.

"Strange kid," Henry muttered to me once Nell was out of earshot.

"Strange? More like great." Any fanboy of TheRuiNar was automatically a good person in my book. Plus, no offense to the rest of my classmates, but they were as lively as zombies on most days. Nell's energy was a welcome change of pace.

Then something occurred to me: Nell would be watching tonight as I entered the third round of qualifiers. The thought made my stomach churn for some reason. I didn't know if I did or *didn't* want him to watch. I mean, what did it matter if he was watching, as long as he didn't know who I really was?

My eyes darted toward Nell, and I caught him staring back at me. Quickly, I turned away and feigned innocence, doing my best to act like I hadn't been looking at him.

"Does someone have a crush on the new kid?" Henry teased.

I blushed. "No! Of course not!"

"Ooooh, I was just asking a question—"

"Henry, do you have to talk so much all the time?" I snapped. He had no idea what was *really* going on.

Henry slunk lower into his seat, which made me feel bad. I mean, Henry had been my best friend since first grade, when we'd instantly bonded over our love of anime and gaming. Henry was also the only friend I'd ever told about Mama's illness.

"Sorry," I mumbled. "I just mean we should be quiet since Professor Kumar's talking now."

Henry flashed me a thumbs-up and mouthed, "All good."

Professor Kumar's lesson today was about Dayhold's core. He handed out some peanut M&M's, which were supposed to illustrate the layers of the Dayhold world or something, but I ate mine too quickly to know what he was going on about. Professor Kumar frowned at me. Oops. Guess I wasn't supposed to eat the M&M.

Ugh. I'd wanted to leave a good impression on my professor— on *all* my professors. Because there were so few female gamers to begin with, I wanted to represent us well. I wanted to stand up for the few girls at my school, too, who were often teased or bullied by the boy students. So I did my best to pay attention in class, but after about five minutes, I could feel my interest slipping. Geography was definitely *not* my favorite subject.

My eyes drifted back in Nell's direction, and I found him squinting at me again. My heart dropped into my stomach. I whipped my head around and did my best to appear as innocent and un-TheRuiNar-like as possible.

I had no idea what the new boy's deal was, but I did know one thing for sure: With Nell around, things at gamer school were about to get a whole lot more interesting.

FOUR

Classes kept everyone busy for the next week after qualifiers. Since this was the last week before the official tournament, our professors had decided that this was the week to cram in all the schoolwork. They knew we'd have the attention span of goldfish once the tournament started. I imagined our teachers sitting in the teachers' lounge, cackling together as they conspired over how to make us students as miserable as possible. It seemed like just the thing they'd do.

"What's the point in memorizing the names of the old white dudes who've worked on developing virtual reality?" grumbled Henry as we left our History of Virtual Reality exam that Friday. My brain was fried from a week of exams. Thankfully, this was the last one. "It's not like that's ever going to help us out during a Dayhold game."

"Shhhh," I hissed. "Professor Nelson can hear you." The professor was frowning at Henry's back.

Henry blushed and muttered in a voice so low only I could hear, "Good. Maybe he'll teach something actually useful next summer camp."

Privately, I kind of agreed, but I was still just grateful to be here, so I didn't say anything.

We entered the cafeteria and headed for the line snaking behind the giant holographic menu. Then a shout came from behind us. "Hey, um, Reyna! And—Harry?"

I turned around at the slightly nervous-sounding voice. It was Nell running to catch up with us. He'd styled his hair like TheRuiNar's again.

"Hi, Nell," I said, with an awkward little wave that I immediately regretted. *Why are you so uncool, Reyna? Get it together. Jeez.*

"I'm Henry, not Harry," corrected Henry, his face pinched in mild annoyance.

"Oh, sorry about that. Hey, that was some exam, huh?" Nell laughed, although the sound came out kind of choked.

"I'll be lucky if I even got half those questions right."

"I'm surprised the professors made you take the exams, since you just got here," I said.

"Well, I did do some learning on my own time at home before I got here," said Nell, grinning.

"Learning? On your own time?" Henry gawked at Nell like he was a strange specimen he'd never seen before. "Why would you do that?"

Nell gave Henry a weird look, like he couldn't understand why Henry *wasn't* learning on his own time.

"Wanna eat with us?" I asked Nell.

He brightened. "Yeah! What's on the menu today? I hope it's something good for us, 'cause I'm getting sick of pizza and hot dogs. You know, for a school with a whole class dedicated to the topic of gaming nutrition, you'd think they'd serve better cafeteria food..."

Henry and I exchanged a look as Nell went off about proper gaming nutrition. I didn't know what to make of Nell just yet, but his enthusiasm for Dayhold was definitely entertaining. We traded Dayhold gamertags, though of course I gave Nell my alt account—ReyningChamp. It's the account I used during class demos or casual games with friends. It sucked to have to play with two accounts, but it kept me and TheRuiNar safe, and that was most important.

Our usual table was taken by a group of gold-level students, so we sat down at a different table. Thirty seconds later, Felix Matthews sauntered over, a few of his tall, intimidating friends flanking him. He glared, and I couldn't help but shrink back. "Hey. You guys are in our spot."

"We got here first," Nell said, frowning.

"You heard Felix. He said you're in our spot. So, move," snapped the blond guy on Felix's right.

Nell looked like he wanted to argue more, but Henry and I gave him a look. We'd both been at summer camp longer than Nell, and we knew the ropes around here. Felix and his crowd set the rules. Nobody dared cross them. Especially not us, the gamers who looked different.

"Anyway, girls like you shouldn't even be here. Go play your dolly dress-up games," snickered the blond guy.

"Forget it," I muttered to Nell. "There's an empty table over there." I pointed. "Let's just go."

The three of us left. Shame shot through me. I knew backing

down was the only thing we could've done. TheRuiNar didn't enter battles that weren't a fair fight.

Later that evening, Henry invited me to hang out in Mimi's room to watch the livestream of the opening ceremony for the Junior Dayhold Tournament. I wrestled with the thought of just making up an excuse to ditch the get-together. Besides Henry, I didn't know the others that well, and strangers made me nervous.

But I decided to put on a brave face and show up, anyway. TheRuiNar always faced challenges head-on. So I, Reyna, had to do that in real life, too.

When I entered Mimi's dorm room, she greeted me with a friendly smile and wave, and then shoved a bag of popcorn into my hand. "Reyna! We've been expecting you. Come in."

Before stepping into Mimi's very pink and very cozy room, I took my shoes off—which was how I'd been raised at home. Mimi, who was also Chinese, had clearly laid down the law with her other guests, since a row of shoes sat right next to the door. Henry waved at me from the bed, where he and Liam were sitting. Liam nodded at me, just once, like he was trying to be cool. (Let's be real, though—when was Liam *not* trying to be cool?)

"You're late," said Liam. "They already showed us the tourna-ment arena, and now it's on to the Fuzion team interview and—"

"Shhhh, Liam. They're talking!" Henry shouted, pointing at Mimi's holographic screen, where the opening ceremony was being broadcast.

I sat down next to Henry on the bed. He scooted over to make room for me, almost knocking Liam off the other end.

"Hey!" Liam scowled at us, but Mimi hushed him.

The ceremony was being broadcast from Fuzion headquarters, where several of the team members were sitting in a huge confer-ence room. A tall, black-haired white man wearing a white dress shirt and black dress pants stood at the end of the table, speaking into a microphone. I recognized him instantly as Commander Dayhold, the founder of the game and president of Dayhold Acad-emy. He was basically a god in the e-sports world. Though it was true that Commander Dayhold *did* catch some flak for being a white man who founded a game that took inspiration from dif-ferent Asian cultures, primarily Chinese—but he also did have Asian game developers who knew what they were doing, so there was that at least.

"...means so much, as always, to have Fuzion give back to

the academy through the Junior Dayhold Tournament," Commander Dayhold was saying to the team. "With your mentorship and support, we're able to host such an ambitious tournament for younger gamers and raise the next generation of Dayholders!"

The team captain, a broad-shouldered, fit blond man who I knew as Marcus Fisher—aka Fisher002, his Dayhold username— spoke into his microphone. He flashed a winning smile toward the cameras. "Of course, Commander Dayhold, none of this would be possible without *your* invention. None of us would even be sitting here in this room! It's only proper that we give back to you and the Dayhold gamer community."

They went on and on complimenting each other for a while. Adults always take so long with their back-and-forth polite nonsense. I found my attention drifting instead toward the two familiar young women sitting side by side at the end of the table. Two of the greatest gamers around, and my heroes in Dayhold.

The woman with a short black pixie cut was Jessica Yoon— LuckyJade847. A Korean American prodigy who'd broken out into the pro Dayhold scene at just seventeen years old, Jessica was really hitting her stride in her career, bagging easy wins for her team left and right.

The brown-haired Mexican American woman next to her, Nina Valdez-Jones—M00nshine—was equally as impressive as Jessica. On a team of almost-all-white male gamers, both women of color stood out.

LuckyJade847 and M00nshine *always* stood out to me. I remembered the moment, over three years ago, when I first saw them battle as part of the Fuzion team. The moment I realized that girls *could* turn pro and game with the best of the guys.

And more importantly, seeing Jessica, an Asian American girl like me, made me realize that *I* could become a pro gamer. Ever since that moment, I'd worked extremely hard. And now here I was on the night before the Junior Dayhold Tournament, where I'd be competing with the best junior gamers around. Shivers of excitement ran down my back.

"Who's your favorite Fuzion team member?" Mimi asked, nudging me.

"I don't think I can choose between LuckyJade847 and M00nshine," I admitted. "You?"

She grinned. "LuckyJade847, because she kinda looks like my

older sister. M00nshine is definitely my second favorite."

"I like the captain the best," Liam offered. "He's, like, invincible in the game."

"What about Sung-Yoon Cho? He's not that flashy, but he's always the one racking up the most points for the team." Henry pointed at the young Korean man sitting to Marcus's left. Sung-Yoon was arguably the best player on the Fuzion team, yet most of the credit for the team's success went to Marcus. It spawned arguments among fans—and many seemed to agree that Sung-Yoon flew under the radar while Marcus got the glory because Marcus was a white male gamer.

"Oh, Sung-Yoon's good, too. But Marcus just *looks* like the best gamer. You know?" Liam flashed us a smile, which we didn't return.

"What do you mean by that?" Mimi asked.

An uncomfortable silence filled the room as Liam faltered under our gazes, his grin disappearing. I had a feeling we all knew what Liam was getting at, even if he couldn't pinpoint it himself. Same reason why Felix Matthews was so popular. Everyone loved the blond-haired white guy gamers. They were basically the face of Dayhold, while players of color were forced into the background.

"This happens so much," Henry mumbled under his breath, but only so I could hear. We exchanged annoyed looks and sighed, much to Liam's confusion.

Henry was half-Japanese and half-white, and the fact that we were both Asian was another reason why we'd stayed friends for years. We just *got* each other. In the Dayhold universe, we faced plenty of thoughtless, racist comments from white gamers, though I also had to struggle with the added layer of sexism. Yay, Dayhold culture.

Mimi shrugged. "I don't think Marcus is that great."

Liam nodded because of *course* now he agreed, and that was that.

The ceremony went on for a while as the players discussed some of the tournament logistics, but I'd already read over the rule book a bazillion times. When I caught myself yawning, I excused myself for being too tired and left for my dorm.

I was exhausted from taking exams and keeping up with two separate Dayhold lives. But unlike the other silver-level students, my work wasn't done yet. The real work started tomorrow at the first official round of the Junior Dayhold Tournament.

The excitement hanging in the air was palpable. Everyone

couldn't stop talking about the start of the tournament. I couldn't tell if I was feeling excited, nervous, or just downright sick.

I'd originally planned to spend the last night before doing some last-minute preparations, like studying old Dayhold livestreams and rereading my class notes from Intermediate Strategy. But instead, I fell asleep as soon as my head hit the pillow.

On Monday morning of the first round, I could feel the difference. I woke up to my alarm going off. Normally I'd snooze it at least two or three times, but not today. Today was too important to sleep in.

The school day seemed to drag on forever. I spent the entire day with my stomach in nervous knots. But then the last classes zipped by in a flash, and before I knew it, it was afternoon, class had ended, and I had a couple hours to prepare.

I rushed back to my room. I took a quick shower and brushed my teeth, bopping to K-pop in my shower to get pumped.

While I dried my hair, I walked over to the holographic screen in front of my bed.

So many great room-service options, but nothing beats breakfast for dinner. My sweet tooth urged me to order a cinnamon roll, but I resisted. What had Professor Nakamura said in my Gaming

Nutrition class? The best pregame food consisted of a mixture of fats, proteins, and carbs. I could practically see the balding old professor turning his perpetual frown on me and my sugar-packed meal.

Sighing, I resisted my cravings and ordered an egg and ham on a bagel instead. "This better launch me to victory," I grumbled.

As the food arrived, the screen in front of my desk flashed to an image of a sharp-faced, ageless man with spiky black hair and a black goatee to match. His eyes glinted. Commander Dayhold. Immediately, I sat up straighter. The commander himself was broadcasting for this tournament. That, more than anything else, made this feel so official and real.

"Good evening, gamers. Tonight's the big night," Commander Dayhold said. "I'm sure you're itching for the first round to begin in just one hour. Before that happens, I'd like to remind you all once again of the rules..."

Commander Dayhold ran over the basic guidelines of the game, as well as the battle royale mode, mostly for the viewers. Dayhold didn't have a storyline. Just different modes and maps for gamers to play. As he spoke, my food arrived, still toasty and perfect.

". . . sudden-death round, where in-game defeat means immediate elimination from the tournament . . ."

I slowly ate the sandwich, savoring the salty taste of the eggs and ham. Focusing on the food was a good way to distract myself from thoughts of the tournament. When I was done eating, I slipped into my green gamer suit, pulled on my white gamer gloves, and secured my VR helmet onto my head.

". . . and as a final reminder, this tournament will be live-streamed to the entire world," said Commander Dayhold.

I gulped. Great. As if I hadn't had enough pressure already sitting on my shoulders.

"You, gamers, are the future of Dayhold. Sponsors and professional Dayhold teams will have their eyes on you. Even those of you who don't win have a very real chance of being scouted right out of this tournament. Don't squander it." Commander Dayhold winked. "Of course, the top priority is still to win."

At his words, I thought of the promise I'd made Mama and Baba. That if I didn't win the whole tournament and bring home the $10,000 cash prize, I would do whatever they wanted me to. Go to engineering or medical school. I would give up on my dream of being a pro Dayhold gamer . . . forever.

My fists clenched at my sides with renewed determination. I couldn't let that happen. A life without Dayhold was unimaginable.

"Remember that your job is to put on your best performance," continued Commander Dayhold, "for the audience in the Dayhold stadium, as well as all the other viewers watching from their homes." After he finished speaking, the video cut to a shot of the Dayhold stadium, a huge, domed indoor structure that I recognized from pro tournaments. The stadium seated 100,000 people, and today it was at least two-thirds full.

My heart thundered in my chest, and sweat gathered in my palms. I'd been playing amateur Dayhold for years, but never in front of an audience of this size. Who knew an amateur tournament could sell out so many seats?

"Now, students. It's the moment you've been waiting for. Training for." A short silence, as though Commander Dayhold wanted his words to sink in. "Just as you did for qualifiers, in five minutes, you'll log in with your Codexes and enter the Dayhold world. This time, you'll be in the first round of the tournament. Take this time for any last-minute preparations. I'll see you on the other side." With a final smile, the image of Commander

Dayhold winked out, replaced with the Dayhold log-in screen.

I did a few stretches, doing my best to shake out the nerves. Audience or not, it didn't matter. I was here to play my best— and win.

I logged in to the game and was taken to a loading screen. Taking deep breaths, I adjusted and readjusted my game suit and headset. I tried to remember everything I'd learned at training camp so far, but my mind had gone unhelpfully blank.

Five minutes were up all too soon. The screen turned green, and then came the familiar yanking sensation around my navel.

It was showtime.

The first round dropped me into a breathtaking scene of the city of Tokyo at night. Huge skyscrapers stretched toward the starless night sky, as far as my helmet-enhanced vision could see. The streets were lined with small shops and restaurants. I'd never been to Japan, but based on what I knew from shows and movies, the Dayhold version of Japan seemed to be pretty accurate. The only difference was that the real Tokyo was a bustling, packed city, but in this world, the streets were empty.

Even though I knew the world around me was entirely virtual, it was hard not to feel like it was real—that my feet were really planted firmly on the ground in Tokyo.

This was no time to stop and admire my surroundings, though. I had a game to win.

I flexed my gamer gloves and took a deep breath. "All right, Codex," I said to my helmet. "Show me any nearby heat sources."

"Showing heat sources," came the robotic reply.

A green screen flashed onto the inside of my visor. I spotted four—no, five—red dots moving rapidly around me, two of them drawing closer.

Fifty, I reminded myself. This was only round one, which meant there were still one hundred gamers standing, and only half would make it to the next round. Fifty gamers had to go down first before I could advance along with forty-nine others.

I thought back to Professor Lucien's lecture from Intermediate Strategy last week. "Each gamer will want to strategize by pacing themselves for the first round," the tall, young, redheaded teacher had said. "Only fifty will advance. In theory, given the sheer number of participants, the first round *should* go quickly. But it won't. It won't go quickly at all. Why not?"

I had known the answer because I'd heard the Fuzion pro

players discuss something similar in a livestream once. "The first round would be the most mentally and physically exhausting round, thanks to the sheer number of enemies that each gamer was up against."

Professor Lucien had given me an appraising look and a rare smile, his gold front tooth glinting in the light. "Thank you. It's exactly as Miss Cheng said." My face had heated with pleasure, and Henry had patted me on the back. "The first round will be the most exhausting. Of course, the final round is also quite taxing for the five gamers who will make it. The main lesson we can all learn is the importance of learning to *pace yourselves*. Use all the resources you have at hand. And no matter what, do *not* panic. Those who get tilted or lose their focus will not recover."

Now the words echoed in my head, particularly this bit: *Use all the resources you have at hand.* Luckily, I'd had plenty of points to exchange for resources. In the past week, I'd stocked up on weapons and special items that might come in handy in battle. I was ready—more than ready for this moment.

In one fluid motion, I placed my messenger bag on the ground. I searched through it, growing frustrated when I couldn't find what I was looking for. Why the heck had I thought that buying this many healing peaches would be a good idea?

Finally, my hand closed over a cold metal shaft. I yanked out my weapon, a wicked double-bladed gray spear that was taller than me. I dug out the weapon just in time. A second later, I heard the sound of a can being kicked down the street, then a flash of red and a sword slicing at me out of nowhere.

Out of instinct, I raised my spear up to block the attack in the nick of time. The resulting clash of metal on metal sent a jolt up my arm that felt way too real. Every time you sustained a hit in-game, you'd feel the jolt of a heavy but cushioned blow from the suit.

The attacker didn't give me a moment to breathe before swinging their sword down and forcing me to block again. Another jolt rocketed up my arms, and I gritted my teeth. Whoever this was had some monstrous reflexes.

Diving out of the way, I held my weapon out in front of me in an attack position as Codex registered the username of the gamer before me.

F3lx, read the holoscript above the gamer's figure.

F3lx: You *are* pretty good, just like everyone's been saying.

TheRuiNar: Everyone?

F3lx: But don't get cocky, newbie. You've got some moves, but I'm better. Sorry 'bout this—gotta take you out early on.

I was so surprised by our interaction, I almost didn't react when F3lx slashed out with his sword again. I was facing F3lx, the number one–seeded player? *Already?* What were the odds?

I raised my spear to block, but not quickly enough—I was going to lose in round one, I couldn't believe it—but then out of nowhere, another gamer rushed at F3lx and knocked him over.

Avenger908, read the username hovering above the new gamer's figure. A speech bubble popped up next to him.

Avenger908: Dirty—rotten—cheater!
F3lx: Just 'cause you suck doesn't make *me* a cheater.

The pair went sprawling onto the ground, punching and kicking at each other as they rolled down the street.

I wish I could say I stayed to finish them both off.

Instead, I fled. I sped off in the opposite direction of the brawling pair, quietly rooting for Avenger908 to take out F3lx. I had no idea if the rumors about his cheating were true, but what I did know for sure was that he was a formidable opponent, and I was totally fine not facing him right now. In fact, if someone else took him out for me, that'd make my life a whole lot easier.

As I turned the corner around a ramen shop, I almost ran smack-dab into a player: a purple-haired guy wearing custom blue battle armor and wielding a sword. Before he could react, I moved quickly. I thought about the feigning tactics Professor Lucien had taught us. I stumbled back, letting this player think that he had me cornered. It worked. He leapt forward, sword raised, but I ducked beneath him. My spear stabbed him in the stomach. He fell with a cry.

I didn't stop to see if my attack had been enough to eliminate the player. I sprinted past, pushing through the aching in my legs. There was no time for stopping. No time for thinking or feeling the exhaustion. Ninety-nine enemies. I had to be one of the fifty still standing by the end of this round. I just had to.

FIVE

Professor Lucien had been right. The first round of the tournament was more grueling than any Dayhold game I'd ever played. The whole ordeal lasted over an hour and was a total bloodbath.

It didn't help that I felt extra pressure. A *lot* of extra pressure. Everything, *everything,* rode on this one tournament. Securing the grand prize was the only way I could help my family pay off all the bills we had, not to mention convince them once and for all that I had the talent to become a top gamer. I couldn't afford to lose.

Codex showed me enemies at every turn, and my instincts, honed from years of battle play, helped me sneak up on and strike down gamers left and right without a thought. One. Two. Three. Four.

But all the while, I couldn't shake off the image of my encounter with F3lx and Avenger908. The way F3lx had moved with a perfect precision that I'd only seen in the gameplay of top pros. The way Avenger908 had charged in and accused F3lx of being dirty.

Were the rumors really true? Was F3lx a cheater?

I was so distracted, I failed to realize how close I was to the nearest gamer until it was too late. A figure leapt out of the shadows. A familiar one, I realized after a moment.

Proslayer: Wait! Um—TheRuiNar!

Proslayer's sudden appearance startled me, but it didn't slow my movement. I whirled around, prepared to face and destroy my attacker—but the black-haired teenage guy was unarmed, holding his hands up in surrender.

Proslayer: Wait—I come in peace this time, I promise. I just want to talk!

Armed or not, Proslayer was an obstacle in the way of me advancing to the second round. I had to wipe him out, just like I'd done during qualifiers, and this time Proslayer would be eliminated from the Junior Dayhold Tournament for good.

No mercy. No hesitation.

That was what I told myself—and yet, when I swung my spear in an arc and Proslayer didn't make a move to defend himself, I stopped my motion mid-swing. He calmly stepped out of my weapon's deadly path.

Was he trying to lure me into a trap? It didn't make sense for him to want to chat with me when he had been so combative during qualifiers.

My eyes narrowed and then flickered from side to side. No heat sources near us. He really seemed to just want to talk. Still, I kept my spear pointed at him. The second he tried any funny business, I'd strike first, without mercy.

TheRuiNar: Make it quick.

Proslayer: Yeah, no worries. I have a proposition. Would you like to team up with me?

That wasn't what I'd been expecting. Actually, I didn't even know what I'd been expecting, but certainly not *that.* Sure, in all likelihood there probably were alliances forming among gamers here and there, but I didn't trust anyone in this tournament as far as I could throw them. It was better to finish this round alone.

I didn't lower my weapon.

TheRuiNar: Why do you want to team up with me?

Proslayer: Because you're one of the best gamers in this tournament, and so am I, and I don't think we need to go head-to-head just yet. Our alliance will only be for this round.

I squinted. There was no way to detect a player's emotion from their avatar, which also made it impossible to tell if they were lying. I had no clue if Proslayer was trying to pull a fast one on me.

Before I could decide what to do, I heard the sound of footsteps pounding the pavement. It was too late to escape. Proslayer and I were surrounded by four other gamers and their weapons, a combination of swords and spears. From the look of it, these four had struck an alliance. I glanced at their usernames. KookiesnKream, Phoenix88, Lazer, and Swolverine. The tournament was open to all, and not every academy student made qualifiers. But I vaguely recalled Lazer as one of the gold-level students and one of F3lx's friends. The idea of taking out this crew now seemed even more appealing.

Swolverine: Dang, boys, look who we have here. TheRuiNar *and* Proslayer.

Phoenix88: The audience will be so shocked when we take them both out in the first round.

Proslayer and I were back-to-back as the gamers circled us. After a quick assessment of the situation, I came to the conclusion that (a) we were cornered and (b) I had no choice but to trust Proslayer, at least until we got out of this mess.

Proslayer: You go left, I'll go right. NOW!

In unison, we dove to either side. The two gamers closest to me were caught off guard by the sudden movement. That was all the opening I needed.

Driving my spear upward, I caught KookiesnKream in the arm with the tip of my weapon, sending him flying backward. He crashed into a nearby noodle shop and didn't get up again.

A second later, his avatar dissolved into nothingness. That was one down.

Swolverine yelled and charged toward me. I blocked his sword with the shaft of my spear. Using my weapon as a springboard, I kicked my feet off the ground and somersaulted through the air, connecting my foot solidly to Swolverine's helmet. As he fell, I landed on all fours, like a cat.

TheRuiNar: What was that about taking me out in the first round?

Before Swolverine could get up, I brought the point of my spear straight into his chest. His gamer suit fizzled, and then he disappeared.

A second one down.

Breathing heavily, I glanced over at Proslayer. With a graceful arc, he turned the last gamer, Phoenix88, into nothing more than pixels. Then he straightened and turned back toward me.

TheRuiNar: All right, you've convinced me, Proslayer. Let's get through this round together.

I couldn't see Proslayer's expression under his helmet, but I'm pretty sure he was smiling.

Readjusting my helmet, I swept my gaze across my surroundings. There seemed to be a lot fewer red dots in our vicinity. I hoped that meant the other gamers were making quick work of each other.

"Codex, how many gamers are still active in this round?" I asked my helmet.

"It is against the tournament rules to answer that question."

I frowned. Should've figured Commander Dayhold would want us to be in the dark. It didn't really make a difference. If Proslayer and I just hung back in this shadowy part of town, we could probably win without doing much more actual fighting ourselves. At the very least, we could buy some time to recover from our battles. That was the textbook response and definitely what Professor Lucien would've told the class to do in a hypothetical situation.

Proslayer: You thinking what I'm thinking?

TheRuiNar: That we should keep charging forward to go finish off the rest of these gamers?

Proslayer: Dude, it's like you read my mind.

In unison, we charged on toward the nearest red dots. After all, hanging back would be no fun. Sorry, Professor Lucien.

Now that we weren't trying to cut each other down, Proslayer and I made a pretty frightening team. I certainly wouldn't have wanted to face us. As we made our way past the virtual dessert shop and video game stores, we eliminated a handful of players. Proslayer fused together a bomb and deployed it on two more players who we found huddling in a dark alley behind a clothing store. The explosion took care of them both instantly.

I knew that we had to be nearing the end of the round—and that the surviving gamers would be a lot more clever and resourceful. Suddenly, I was glad to have a strong gamer like Proslayer on my side to watch out for the danger that even my Codex-enhanced vision couldn't catch.

I craned my neck around a corner but immediately stepped back, bumping into Proslayer.

Proslayer: What is it?

TheRuiNar: Gamers. Two of them. I think one of them is F3lx.

Proslayer: Impossible. We'd have sensed them on our Codexes.

How—

A sword came hurtling at us from around the corner. I ducked to the side in the nick of time, diving out of its reach. Proslayer reacted quickly, too, raising his sword to parry his attacker's. F3lx. I swear, this dude was *everywhere*.

Proslayer: Too slow!

With lightning speed, F3lx dove toward Proslayer again. I leapt to my feet to rush to Proslayer's aid but found my path blocked by the second gamer, whose username was PrdOtaku.

I raised my spear just as he drove his downward. Our weapons clashed. My arm jolted from the impact. Hits like this affected my in-game health. I had to do whatever it took to keep PrdOtaku from stabbing me.

I thought about my messenger bag—just out of reach while I was holding my defensive position. If I could grab a peach, I could power up, restore my energy levels, and finish this guy off with one blow.

PrdOtaku suddenly went flying sideways. It took a second for me to realize that Proslayer had tackled him from the side. This was the chance I'd been waiting for.

I grabbed the first peach my fingers touched in my messenger bag, and ate it immediately.

"Health levels restored by fifty percent," my Codex said.

Heat and strength surged inside me. I stood, ready to charge into battle.

But before I could move, F3lx stabbed Proslayer right in his back.

TheRuiNar: NOOOOOOO!

I tried to charge, but my body was frozen in shock. Proslayer turned toward me. I couldn't see his expression, but my imagination conjured one up for me: shock, realization, rage, sadness.

Then my lone in-game ally dissolved into nothingness.

I'd only teamed up with Proslayer briefly for this round, but there was something about him that had struck me as familiar—and comforting. Now that he was gone, I felt completely, utterly alone. And furious. I pointed my spear at F3lx and PrdOtaku.

TheRuiNar: You'll pay for that!

But before any of us could make a move, the world froze. Commander Dayhold's voice announced over my helmet, "Congratulations, gamers. The fiftieth player has just been eliminated. You've all made it to the second round of the Junior Dayhold Tournament!"

SIX

After leaving the world of Dayhold and returning to my dorm, I barely had the energy left to scarf down a second, late dinner before I knocked out. I slept all the way through my alarm and was late to my first class the next day, A History of Virtual Reality.

From the look of it, though, I wasn't the only one who'd had a hard time getting out of bed this morning. A few students trickled in after me, and a few didn't show up at all. Henry wasn't here, either, but that was because he had an appointment with the guidance counselor to discuss career plans.

I tried paying attention to Professor Nelson's lecture, but it was hard to summon the energy to listen to the mechanics of Dayhold engineering on a normal day. The day after the brutal beating my body had taken during the first round of the tournament?

Forget it. It was a miracle that I managed to stay awake at all.

I was so tired, I almost didn't notice Nell come up to me after the class.

"Hey, Reyna."

Blinking the sleep out of my eyes, I found myself facing a smiling Nell, who was bouncing up and down on the balls of his feet. I'd give anything to have this kid's energy right now. With how sore my legs were from the workout they got yesterday, I was pretty sure I wouldn't be bouncing casually like that for a while.

"Hey, Nell. What's up?"

His eyes darted away from mine and then back. Unless I was mistaken, he seemed shy. I couldn't help but smile at the thought. "Um, I was just wondering if you wanted to sit together at lunch. Again."

Aww. He *was* nervous. Maybe he was worried about sitting alone at a school where he didn't really know anybody yet. I wasn't sure why he seemed to like me so much—a lot of guys at school actually went out of their way to sit away from the girls—but I didn't mind. I liked Nell, too, even if he was a little strange.

"Sure. That's cool with me. You can sit with me whenever you want."

Nell's eyes lit up, and he beamed. "Awesome. Man, I hope they serve the spaghetti and meatballs that they made yesterday."

"If the cafeteria serves the same food as yesterday, you can bet they'll be all stale," I warned.

"Oh." His face fell. "I guess that makes sense . . ." Nell shook his head. "Forget about the food, though. Did you watch the livestream for the tournament last night? There was a watch party in the commons room, but I didn't go. TheRuiNar pulled off this really sweet feint on one of the players. It was, like, straight out of Professor Lucien's lessons."

At the sudden mention of my feint, I was so thrown that I tripped over nothing. Thankfully, I caught myself by steadying my body on a nearby wall.

Nell gave me a funny look. "You good, Reyna?"

I had to change the subject. "Um, yeah. Totally. Just tripped on the—um— Hey, I'm starving, aren't you? Let's hurry to lunch!" I grabbed Nell's arm before he could interrupt, and we rushed for the cafeteria. Phew. I needed to get better at acting natural whenever someone brought up the Junior Dayhold Tournament, 'cause that was gonna happen a *lot.*

As Nell and I entered the packed room, we joined the back of the food line. I cast a look around at my classmates and heard snatches of conversation here and there about the first round.

"Did you see—"

"*Proslayer* got knocked out. I totally didn't see that coming."

"—and at the end—"

"So, you're from California, right?" I said to Nell to fill in the awkward silence.

His head bobbed up and down. "Yup. Sacramento."

"Cool. Is Dayhold really popular there, too?" I thought back to Nell's introduction to our class during Dayhold Geography, and how he'd already known about TheRuiNar, despite the fact that I was still an emerging figure in the amateur Dayhold circuits.

"Yeah, Dayhold's pretty popular where I grew up. My dad is a retired pro player, actually. So he's still super invested in the game. He flies me out to the Midwest and the East Coast just to watch pro tournaments."

"Wow." My eyebrows rose. The way Nell had casually blurted that out about his father flying him around the country told me he probably came from a wealthy family. It wasn't a surprise to me, though. Most of the students at the academy were paying a hefty tuition to learn from pros about the elite sport. Unlike me, here on scholarship. I couldn't relate to the rich kids, and hearing about their fancy gadgets or families' private villas only made me more aware of how much I lacked. How out of place I was among Dayhold gamers.

"When did your father retire?" I asked.

"It was a few years ago. Right when Dayhold was getting mega popular. Oh, and you wouldn't have heard of Dad," Nell said when I opened my mouth to ask my next question. "He was in the minor leagues. He retired because he aged out. And because . . . well, the other players weren't very . . . nice to him."

I could guess from Nell's downcast, forlorn figure what he meant by "weren't very nice." There were plenty of stories about industry racism circulating on the internet.

"But enough talk about me," Nell said after a moment of silence, waving his hand through the air. "Did you see TheRuiNar's moves last night? That dude is *awesome*. Totally smoked the whole competition."

I didn't think I'd *smoked* the competition, but I knew I'd played well. Hearing Nell's praise made my heart lift. "Hey, how'd you become a fan of TheRuiNar, anyway?"

"Ooh. I told you my dad takes me to tournaments, right? Well, he took me to this amateur tournament last year—the Spring Dayhold Games?"

"Oh yeah, I've heard of that." I tried to appear casually interested, hiding the truth.

"Come to think of it, I think that was the first time TheRuiNar appeared in a public tournament," Nell said thoughtfully, rubbing his chin. "Don't remember hearing anything about him before."

Nell was right about that. Before the Spring Dayhold Games, I'd never entered any kind of tournament.

"Anyway, I thought TheRuiNar *rocked*. He took third place, but if you ask me, he should've gotten first. After that tournament, I started following TheRuiNar's livestreams. He never talks and he doesn't stream that much, but when he does, he's amazing."

I willed my face not to turn red, but my cheeks were definitely getting a little heated from all of Nell's praise. A small part of me wondered what would happen if I just came out and said it to Nell—admitted that *I* was TheRuiNar. He'd be totally shocked. He might even lose respect for TheRuiNar once he realized his favorite amateur gamer was . . . me.

I couldn't tell Nell or Henry the truth. Neither of them had ever been in my shoes as a girl gamer, and I didn't think even they would understand what it was like for me.

"TheRuiNar is going to be famous one day, and I'll get to say I was his number one fan from the start," Nell was saying. He puffed out his chest. "Oh, and you can be his number two fan, Reyna."

I grinned. "Sounds like a plan."

We ordered and grabbed our food—leftover spaghetti and meatballs, as I'd predicted, which made Nell groan—and found Henry, back from his appointment with the counselor, sitting at our usual table. We sat down and ate lunch, with Nell still going on and on about his favorite Dayhold tournaments he'd been to with his dad. Being with my friends and talking about what we loved most, my heart felt lighter than it had in days.

The light feeling didn't last. After a long day of classes, I had homework to finish for a few of my professors, but luckily it didn't take long. I guess they were being merciful since they knew the Junior Dayhold Tournament was going on.

When I finished drawing a quick map for my Dayhold Geography assignment, I glanced toward my holographic screen. Normally, I'd relax by playing a round of Dayhold as

ReyningChamp with my friends for fun, but the idea of practicing now made me more anxious than anything else. Plus, I wanted to save my strength for tomorrow evening, when I'd have to show off my stuff during the second round of the Dayhold tournament. Instead of practicing, I let myself relax—sort of—by stocking up on fresh items from the Dayhold store.

I had almost two thousand points to spend now, which was the most money I'd ever had thanks to last night. All my frugality went out the window. There was no point in holding back when the other gamers were probably going on a spending spree to snag themselves the best weapons. No way was I going to be left in the dust.

I bought a few swords and shields, not to mention enough healing peaches for a whole army. There were other in-game items that caught my eye—healing potions and traps—but I ignored them in favor of using my precious points to upgrade my favorite weapon, the Ruyi Jingu Bang. I made it longer, slimmer, and easier to wield, powerful enough to take out two foes at the same time.

Just as I'd decided to turn in early for the night—I was still exhausted from the first round—my monitor screen glowed with an incoming video call. The caller ID flashing on the screen— *HOME*—reminded me of something important.

"I forgot to call yesterday!" I groaned. And I'd almost forgotten to call tonight, too. My parents were going to be so mad.

Turning down the volume on the monitor, I picked up the call. The faces of my parents winked onto the screen. There was Baba, with his short black hair streaked with gray, wrinkles lining his face. And Mama sitting beside him, her slightly curly black hair falling to her shoulder. She wore a tired smile. Behind my parents was the TV, so I could tell they were calling from the living room.

"H-hello," I said, already dreading the incoming lecture.

"Rui Na." Baba was right on cue with a stern voice. He frowned. "Why didn't you call yesterday?"

"Sorry, Baba," I mumbled. "Um . . . I was really busy." It was the truth, after all.

"Busy? What could possibly keep you so busy that you'd forget to call home?"

Ah, the classic guilt trip, aka Baba's favorite move.

"Rui Na was busy with summer camp, of course!" Mama huffed, turning to Baba with a frown. He shrunk back a little and pursed his lips. Luckily, I could usually count on my mother to come to my defense whenever my father started to scold me. Mama turned to me. "Are you having fun at the academy?"

"Yeah, lots of fun! Yesterday was the first round of the Junior Dayhold Tournament," I explained. "I played all day, and I was so tired that I fell asleep right after the round. Oh, and I made it past the first round, too!"

"That's wonderful! Isn't it?" she prompted my father.

Baba was silent for a moment. I held my breath, hoping—waiting—for my father to praise me. To tell me he was proud that I'd made it past the first round. If he showed even a tenth of Nell's enthusiasm, I'd be happy.

"You should've still found time to check in with us," my father said, his voice as stiff as ever. Not even a shred of enthusiasm in his words, nor a hint of a smile on his face. "Do you know how worried your mother and I were when we didn't hear from you?"

My shoulders drooped. I should've known it was a wasted hope. Unlike Mama, Baba didn't praise me. That just wasn't his style. I considered myself lucky if I could hold a five-minute conversation with my father without him scolding me.

"I said sorry," I mumbled.

"And—wait. You were so exhausted that you fell asleep right after the round? That doesn't sound healthy. Are you being mistreated there?"

"You're *not* being mistreated, right?" Mama chimed in, narrowing her eyes.

"What? No! Nobody's been mistreating me." I paused. "Well, sometimes the gamers can be kinda sexist toward girls . . ."

Baba sighed. "I'm not surprised. That's one of the reasons I tried to warn you about gaming, Rui Na. Have any of the boys been giving you a hard time?"

"No . . . nobody specifically," I mumbled.

"How is the academy otherwise?"

"Great!" I had to talk up the school, otherwise they would really think I was being mistreated here and they'd want to come take me home immediately. "I mean, the students here—especially those of us in the tournament—are treated like royalty. I even get room service." Baba and Mama exchanged a serious, meaningful look. Uh-oh. I recognized that look. It meant bad news for me.

Baba said, "There's something we have to tell you. Something very, very important." His voice had grown, if possible, even more serious and grave.

"Wh-what is it?" Suddenly, I was nervous.

"Your mother . . . The doctor called today to say that her condition has worsened."

Mama cast her gaze down.

"Oh." I didn't know what else to say.

"I've decided to undergo surgery," Mama said in a small voice.

"Rui Na, I think it's best if you leave the academy and come back home," said Baba. My mother cut him a look, but he frowned at her. "What?"

They started to argue over whether I should come home or not, but I'd already tuned out the conversation, sitting back numbly on my bed. My heart sunk to the floor and then right through it. On Professor Kumar's map of Dayhold, my heart would be buried deep in Dayhold's core.

"What kind of surgery?" I asked.

"It's called a mastectomy," Mama explained.

I had no idea what that was, but it seemed like it'd be painful. "Wh-what's a m-m-mastectomy?"

"It removes all the breast tissue to help fight the breast cancer."

I shuddered, picturing Mama, all alone in a white hospital, surrounded by scary-looking, painful instruments.

"It won't be that bad," Mama said in a reassuring voice. "I didn't even want to tell you, but your father *insisted*..." She shot him a reproachful look.

"I'm sorry, Rui Na." Baba didn't look sorry at all. "But I think you're old enough to handle the truth, without sugarcoating. Your mother needs surgery at the end of the weekend."

"*This* week?" I yelped. That was so soon. Another surgery meant another bill to worry about, on top of worrying about the actual procedure going well for Mama. And the tournament finals were happening on Sunday!

"It would be in all of our interests if you left this silly gamer dream behind, Rui Na," Baba said, his voice quiet but stern. "I know you want to win the grand prize to help pay off the bills, and that's very courageous of you. However, your mother and I would prefer you stay at home and study something more useful, like math or science. That way, in the future, you'll make lots of money and be able to support yourself and a family. It'll be easier on you as well. Being an Asian gamer ... well, Dayhold isn't really your place. You'll understand one day."

"You're being too harsh on Rui Na," Mama scolded, and that spawned another argument between my parents.

Tears pooled in my eyes. Even though my brain told me my father's words made the most logical sense, my heart still longed to play on a pro Dayhold team. Even if I had to fight gamers who didn't think girls had the chops to make it.

I wasn't like Baba. I wasn't good at math or science. Dayhold was the one thing I excelled at, but my father just saw it as a waste of time.

"Can . . . can you give me a day to decide?" It took all my remaining willpower to speak steadily, without letting my voice break, even though all I wanted to do was cry. "Tomorrow is the second round of the tournament. I want to play one more round, at least."

"Rui Na—" Dad started to scold, but then seemed to hold himself back. The audio crackled with the sound of him blowing a breath. The angry redness in his cheeks slowly faded as he released a sigh. "Fine. One more round. Then you come home."

"Wait, that's not what I—"

Click. The video call ended abruptly. My parents had hung up, and I was left to stand there staring at the blank screen. Stunned. Numb.

A few things had become certain—our family needed money for Mama's medical bills now more than ever, and if I messed up during this tournament, I'd lose the chance to help my family *and* fulfill my gaming dreams.

SEVEN

I had never awoken in less of a mood to game. But the tournament certainly wasn't going to wait for a twelve-year-old girl with family problems to get her act together. So the next morning, I let my alarm snooze only once and then pulled back the curtains to reveal a gloomy, rainy sky.

"Great," I sighed. "Not even the weather's on my side." It wasn't like the weather of the outside world was going to affect my game-play in the virtual reality world of Dayhold, but seeing gray skies first thing in the morning certainly didn't help.

I'd barely gotten a wink of sleep last night. I think I dozed off for an hour at around three or four a.m., but I'd tossed and turned in my sheets for the majority of the night, worried. Worried about my mother. Worried about what my family was going to do about this new hospital bill, on top of all our other bills, especially if I abruptly packed up my things and pulled out of the tournament with empty pockets.

In the Dayhold universe, TheRuiNar was the picture of confidence and lived up to that image well. Never backing down from a battle. Never losing a fight. But Rui Na, who lived in the real world, was so ... not that. Sometimes, even *I* wasn't totally sure that I was the one behind TheRuiNar.

My gloomy mood didn't improve throughout the school day, even though Nell and Henry did their best to try to cheer me up. I wasn't sure how I made it through my classes, but soon enough it was early evening again—aka time to game.

Trying to boost my mood, I blasted K-pop in my room. The upbeat songs made me smile, but only just a little.

Since this was potentially my last time ordering room service at Dayhold Academy, I got cinnamon rolls. I regretted my decision when I'd eaten my third roll and got a bad stomachache from stuffing my face too quickly. Why did sugar have to taste *so* good?

As I was struggling to get into my black gamer suit, the computer screen lit up with Commander Dayhold's face. He was smiling, as always. "Good evening, Dayholders. Congratulations again on making it to the second round of the Junior Dayhold Tournament. This round will follow the same battle royale format as the first round, but with fewer players. Twenty-five gamers will be eliminated, and twenty-five will advance to the third round."

Twenty-five was a lot fewer than one hundred, where we'd started at just two days ago. The whirlwind pace of the tournament was enough to make my head spin.

"Once again, this round will be broadcast to the live audience at the Dayhold stadium"—the footage cut from Commander Dayhold's face to a shot of the packed crowd, and then cut back to the commander's face—"as well as to those who are tuning in from the comfort of their own homes. So do your best, gamers. The world is cheering you on!"

Knowing that added more pressure and made me extra nervous, though Commander Dayhold had probably intended his words to be motivational. I pulled on my gamer gloves. I didn't need the world to cheer me on or watch me mess up. The cinnamon rolls in my stomach threatened to make a reappearance. I tried to calm myself down by focusing on the newest techniques we'd learned in Intermediate Strategy, picturing myself making the motions.

"That's enough rambling from me, though," said Commander Dayhold. "I'm sure you're all very eager to get on with this round. The battle begins in five minutes. Please log in, and good luck, Dayholders!"

Deep breaths, Reyna. I closed my eyes and inhaled for a long beat, and then exhaled. Inhale. Exhale. Repeat. After a few minutes passed, I could feel it working—my heart rate slowing, the nervous knot in my stomach untangling. Without letting myself think too much, I logged in to the Dayhold system.

Moments later, I was being beamed into the Dayhold universe again. With a flash of light, I landed on all fours in something grainy and soft that slipped through my fingers. Sand.

I looked up and quickly assessed my surroundings. White sand. Tall palm trees swaying in the breeze. Sparkling ocean water under a cloudless blue sky, stretching as far as the eye could see. For the third round of the tournament, we were going to be battling on an island.

I shook myself out of my reverie. If I got distracted by pretty sights now, I'd be struck down by an enemy gamer faster than I could say "paradise."

"Codex, show me any heat sources nearby," I commanded. My

helmet obeyed, and I noticed that most of the pulsing red dots were a ways off from me. But there was one that appeared to be really close, just slightly off to my left.

This unfortunate gamer was going to be TheRuiNar's first opponent.

From the depths of my messenger bag, I drew out my favorite weapon: the new and improved Ruyi Jingu Bang. Playing Dayhold just wasn't the same if I didn't use the mighty red-and-gold staff, after all. Wielding the weapon behind my back, I crouched beneath the swaying trees. My eyes tracked the heat source as it drew closer to me. As soon as the player got within attack range, I would strike them down before they even knew what hit them.

Then my hand stilled on my staff as a thought occurred to me. During the first round, Proslayer and I had teamed up, and it had gone pretty well—aside from the part where he got eliminated. There was no rule against teaming up in this round, either, which meant the other gamers were probably already forming alliances. And if they all formed alliances, where did that leave me?

Battling those alliances, all on my own.

No thanks. I was good, but I didn't think I was *that* good.

The red dot drew nearer, and the rustling of leaves told me that the gamer was right under my nose. Before I could change my mind, I leapt out of my hiding spot.

TheRuiNar: Hey! Don't attack. I, um, I come in peace.

Note to self: Come up with a better opener next time.

The gamer turned around, and I was taken aback to see that she was a girl. She had braided black hair and dark brown skin. I couldn't assume that this gamer was a girl in real life just because the avatar was. How did I know this person wasn't just a guy who wanted to use a girl avatar? They were free to do that more than we could. The bubble above her head told me her username was RHCP. She wielded two curved, short swords, and assumed a threatening position with them placed in front of her chest.

RHCP: Oh yeah? What's to stop me from attacking you, TheRuiNar?

TheRuiNar: Listen, in the first round of this tournament, there were plenty of alliances. I'm sure you noticed. Maybe you were even part of an alliance yourself.

She gave no indication to confirm this one way or another.

TheRuiNar: Uh, so, I think it'd be a good idea if you and I teamed up. Plus, we're both great gamers.

I was sure I'd seen the username RHCP among the top finishers during the qualifying rounds. If we struck an alliance, it'd make the odds of both of us making it out of here much higher.

RHCP: Mmmm. You wouldn't be my top choice, but I suppose you'll do.

TheRuiNar: Not your top choice?

RHCP: Yeah, no, sorry. Top choice would be F3lx. He's a heck of a player, and whoever teams up with him will definitely make it to the third round.

TheRuiNar: Well, I think we can take on F3lx—and anyone else—without cheating.

RHCP shrugged and lowered her weapons. She transferred both swords to her left hand, and then held out her right hand for a virtual handshake. I grabbed it and shook, sealing the alliance.

RHCP: Cool. Let's go take down some gamers.

I let RHCP lead as we made our way through the trees, using nature as our cover. I told her I was guarding her back. But truthfully, I had another reason for wanting to stay behind RHCP—I wanted to make sure she couldn't stab me in the back, literally. I wasn't taking any chances, especially not on a hastily arranged alliance with a gamer who didn't seem to mind foul play in Dayhold. To be extra careful, I drew my metal shield out of my bag. Even though it was rather heavy and unwieldy and would slow me down in battle, it was excellent self-defense against sudden, unexpected attacks. Like I said—I wasn't taking *any* chances.

My Codex showed me that we were drawing closer to what I guessed was another duo of gamers, based on how closely the two dots were spaced together.

RHCP stopped abruptly on the path, causing me to bump into her.

TheRuiNar: Ow! Why'd you stop?

RHCP: Do you hear that?

I strained my ears. The rustling of leaves. The snapping of branches underfoot. The two dots were way closer to us now, I realized with a spike of nervousness. How had they moved so quickly? Maybe the island was smaller than I'd realized.

Then—

Arrows shot at us out of a cluster of bushes. Quicker than I could think, I raised my shield in front of RHCP and me, and the arrows thudded against it. Now I was really glad I'd brought it out earlier.

Then the pair of gamers we'd been tracking dove at us out of the bushes on our left. I veered out of the way quickly, in the same movement drawing both my shield and the Ruyi Jingu Bang in front of me for protection.

I didn't even have time to register the nearest gamer's username before he was on me, notching an arrow into his bow. His mistake. The bow and arrow was a great weapon—from a distance. With close combat, he didn't stand a chance. Especially not against me, armed with my favorite and best weapon.

I stabbed upward with the Ruyi Jingu Bang. The staff knocked his bow out of his hands. While he was off balance, I didn't give him even a moment to catch his breath before spinning the staff around and slamming it against his back. The gamer fell to his knees, and I looked away as he disintegrated.

"Plus three hundred points," Codex said.

A second scream told me the other gamer had been eliminated, too. I glanced over at RHCP, who was bent over at the knee, panting and wiping some dirt off her gamer suit.

TheRuiNar: Hey, we make a pretty solid team.

RHCP straightened until we were standing helmet-to-helmet. Right now was one of those moments where I really, really wished I could read the expressions on my fellow gamers' faces.

RHCP: Yeah. You're really strong.

TheRuiNar: Oh. Thanks. You too.

RHCP: That's why I'm extra sorry to do this. But if I don't put an end to you now, you'll cause problems for me down the road.

Then RHCP stabbed me in the neck.

EIGHT

Or she *would* have, if I didn't lift my shield up to block the attack. I guess she'd never learned that "teamwork makes the dream work."

I used my shield to shove RHCP away with all my strength, until she stumbled into a nearby bush. I leapt several feet back, out of the way.

The betrayal didn't really come as a shock to me. I'd expected it and stayed ready to defend myself accordingly. I just hadn't expected RHCP to attack me *this* quickly.

A second later, RHCP emerged from the bush and dusted off her gamer suit.

RHCP: Well, I guess it wouldn't be interesting if you didn't dodge that.

She didn't seem at all put off by the fact that her sneak attack had failed.

I stayed silent. We circled each other slowly, like hawks, or maybe two people trapped in a bizarre dance. The trees, the island, the trail underfoot—all our surroundings disappeared, until it was just RHCP and me. The tension in the air grew unbearably thick.

I struck first. RHCP countered my Ruyi Jingu Bang by raising both of her swords up as a shield. *Clang!* Metal clashed on metal. RHCP pushed against my staff. I gritted my teeth and dug my shoes into the ground, my arm trembling with the force of pushing her back.

RHCP: Is that all you've got? I'm disappointed.

In one motion, she shoved me. I stumbled and crashed into the bushes.

By the time I righted myself and landed out of the bushes on all fours, RHCP hovered above me, her two swords glinting in the sunlight. Yet again, I couldn't help but marvel at how realistic the virtual reality world of Dayhold was.

RHCP: Any last words, TheRuiNar?

TheRuiNar: Yeah. Mind your neck.

I drew my right fist and then punched in an uppercut, connecting solidly with her chin. The force of my punch sent an off-balance RHCP tumbling down a small hill. I didn't give her a chance to recover. I leapt to my feet and pinned her down to the ground by standing on her neck with my right foot, my Ruyi Jingu Bang raised to deliver a final, fatal blow.

TheRuiNar: Any last words, RHCP?

RHCP: Mind *your* neck next round. F3lx isn't playing clean.

I waited, but she didn't add anything else. Without pausing to think of what this warning meant, I swung my staff down in an arc, and RHCP disappeared beneath my foot.

Another gamer down. I did my signature victory dance, going through the motions, but felt no joy this time. My mind raced. Yet another gamer accusing F3lx of cheating. F3lx was quickly becoming a bigger and bigger nuisance, and I had the feeling that I had to take him down before he took me out.

I checked my Codex for any nearby heat sources. There was a duo of red dots nearby, I assumed from a pair of gamers who'd decided to team up. If it was just the two of them, then I was pretty sure I at least had a shot of taking them down.

As swiftly as I could, I moved from bush to bush. Since I didn't have the element of surprise on my side, I had to use my speed to my full advantage. The duo spun toward me just as I reached striking distance. Evidently, their Codex scan had told them an enemy gamer was right on their heels.

I raised my staff and used it to slash through a tree branch in my way. But before I could engage the duo in battle, a *third* gamer leapt out of the nearby trees: F3lx!

F3lx swung his sword at my head, but I recovered my wits just in time to dive out of the way. My palms and knees hit the ground, and I gritted my teeth as skin scraped rocks. What was with F3lx and his ability to show up at the worst times?

Leaping to my feet, I ignored the sharp pain shooting up my arms and legs and sprinted back toward the battle. But the only gamer who stood in the clearing now was F3lx; the duo had disappeared. After a moment, I registered what this meant— that F3lx had easily taken down the other two gamers in the span of time that I'd been gathering myself from my fall.

F3lx turned his weapon on me, and I raised my staff. Now I was more determined than ever to be the one to bring him down. As I prepared to strike, I suddenly realized my arms and legs were no longer responding to me. A strange, cold sensation trickled through my body, from the top of my head down to the tips of my toes. I was totally frozen. Totally helpless, right in F3lx's warpath.

F3lx shifted forward, and—then his body froze, too.

Before either of us could make a move, the familiar red message board materialized in front of us, signaling the end of the round.

Commander Dayhold's voice came over my helmet. "With the twenty-fifth elimination, the second round of the Junior Dayhold Tournament has concluded. Congratulations to the twenty-five gamers remaining. You're through to the third round—the semifinals!"

The world around us began to dissolve, but not before F3lx got in one last word.

F3lx: See you in the semis, TheRuiNar.

I didn't get a chance to reply before the familiar jerking sensation occurred in my navel, and then the virtual reality world of Dayhold was gone. I was back in my dorm, gazing up at the posters of my idols, LuckyJade847 and M00nshine.

The first thing I did was click into the livestreamed footage of the finished round and glance over the comments, even though I knew I probably shouldn't.

Anon457: Lol I'm not surprised that RHCP got knocked out this round. I'm just surprised she lasted this long tbh.

Anon70: Yeahhh lmao more proof girls are awful gamers.

Anon02: This is why girls shouldn't be in e-sports.

My blood boiled. I wasn't surprised to see the horrible comments directed at RHCP. A quick online search of the username RHCP brought up a few different images of different girls. I didn't know which one was RHCP, and I assumed the gamer had hidden her true identity for safety purposes. Now I was even angrier. Stuff like this was exactly why I hid the fact that I was a girl. RHCP was brave, staying true to herself despite all the awful insults. Braver than me.

Finally, I forced myself to tear my gaze away from the screen. It wasn't until a full thirty minutes later, after I'd exited the world of Dayhold and was lying down on my bed staring at the ceiling, that the realization hit me.

I'd made it through to the third round, somehow. I'd made it by the skin of my teeth. I was going to *semifinals*.

I sat up and shook my head, trying to cast off the sudden dizzy spell. I couldn't tell what I was feeling. Happiness? Uncertainty? Shock? Probably a mixture of all of the above, plus a sugar crash from eating all those cinnamon rolls earlier. Note to self: No more eating pastries right before important battles.

Although I was so close to the $10,000 grand prize now I could almost taste it, I wasn't in the mood to celebrate at all. Being back in the real world reminded me of the reality of my real-world problems, all in a rush. Mama's surgery. Baba asking me to pull out of the academy and the tournament.

If I ignored Baba's request, and stayed at school and finished the tournament, that would make me a bad daughter. So the responsible thing to do would be to abandon the tournament, let go of my pro dreams, and go home.

But I'd already come so far in the tournament. Victory was

right within reach. Go home and be with my father and sick mother? Or stay and finish the tournament and continue my Dayhold dreams? Go home. Or stay here. The impossibility of the forked path before me made my head pound and my heart ache. No matter what I chose to do, I was going to have to leave behind something—or someone—important to me.

Staring up at the posters of my idols, I sighed. Those women were so strong and amazing. Not just because they were some of the best pro players around, the stars of Fuzion, but also because they were always speaking out against the misogyny in the gamer world.

"What would you do if you were in my place?" I asked. "Would you choose duty to your family or duty to yourself?"

LuckyJade847 and M00nshine stared back at me, silent, with smiles frozen.

NINE

The tournament had me so physically and mentally exhausted. My heart threatened to shatter into a million pieces, but I knew what I had to do. I turned on my monitor screen and dialed my home number.

It picked up on the fourth ring. My father stared at me from the living room. I'd clearly caught him right after work, because he was still wearing a blue dress shirt and black work pants. "Rui Na?"

"Baba. I finished the second round in the tournament. I . . . I made it through to the third round."

"Oh." My father didn't sound that surprised, but he didn't sound that happy, either. His expression was stoic, as usual. I might have just told him the weather. "Good job."

Wow. I was so taken aback by Baba's rare compliment,

I almost forgot to reply. "Th . . . thanks. Where's Mama?"

"She's sleeping. She gets tired easily these days." Baba paused. "You're still coming home, right? I can call the commander to pull you out of the academy, and I can drive you home tomorrow. You'll make it in time for your mother's surgery."

I squeezed my eyes shut. For some reason, an image of Nell's and Henry's smiling faces appeared in my mind, and a lump formed in my throat. My friends. They still had no idea about anything that was going on with me. Was this really going to be goodbye?

"I . . ."

"Leaving gamer school is definitely for the best," Baba was saying. "Gaming is . . . well, it isn't well suited for people like us."

"People like us?"

"People who aren't . . . white."

That much was already obvious to me, even though I'd only been watching and playing Dayhold for a few years. Even though I got that Baba wanted to protect me, I couldn't help but feel annoyed. But I didn't know what to say back. After all, he was right.

Baba's eyebrows knitted together with concern. "If you come home quickly, we can still sign you up for math camp, too. You can get ahead of your classmates for the upcoming school year."

Math camp. I shuddered. Was there anything worse?

"Gaming is also too dangerous for a girl like you."

Annoyance spiked in me. How many times had I heard a version of those words since I'd started playing Dayhold? My eyes flickered back toward the posters of LuckyJade847 and Moonshine on my wall. There weren't many pro female gamers, but they *did* exist. And they were so talented. They were my heroes.

When I'd first showed a love for gaming a few years back, Mama had gone out and spent precious dollars on these posters of female gamers. She'd printed out newspaper articles about LuckyJade847 and M00nshine for me to read, too. Remembering this made me ache terribly for my mother. Out of my parents, she'd been the more understanding of my love for Dayhold.

Wait a minute. Baba wanted me to come home to be there while my mother's illness worsened. He wanted me to be there for the surgery. But he'd never told me what *Mama* wanted.

Somehow, deep down in my heart, I already knew what my mother would want me to do, even though she was ill.

And I had a feeling that if my Dayhold heroes had been in my shoes, they'd do the same thing, too.

"Dayhold is too violent for a young girl to play, and—"

"You're wrong," I blurted without thinking.

Silence. Uh-oh. I'd never talked back to Baba like that before. He was definitely going to let me have it now.

"Rui Na!" my father shouted, sounding aghast.

But suddenly, I realized, I didn't have to listen to my father, like the good girl I'd always been. I didn't have to leave the academy and go home.

It wasn't like my parents were paying my tuition to the academy. That money came from the scholarship that I'd earned using my gaming skills.

"What's all the noise? Is Rui Na calling?"

Baba and I both glanced behind him, where my mother had come into the living room. She'd clearly just woken up. Her hair was still in its curlers, and she wore her plain gray nightgown.

"Go back to sleep," Baba said, trying to wave off my mother, but she dodged him and came up close to the video screen.

"Mama, shouldn't you be resting?" I asked. "Don't you have your surgery this weekend?"

My mother flashed a smile, but she couldn't disguise the

exhaustion in her features. "I'm all right, bǎo bèi. The doctor is hopeful I'll have the strength to pull through."

Seeing Mama appear so weak made me rethink. Maybe I *should* be there for her, after all. Even if it meant missing the tournament. "That's good. I should be there for your surgery. I should see if I can get out of camp somehow—"

"No, Rui Na."

I blinked. "What?"

"I don't want you to worry about me. In fact, I forbid it." A cough. I heard my father's worried voice start to say something to Mama, but she spoke over him. "You have to concentrate on your gaming. You've worked so hard to attend this camp!"

"But Mama . . . Baba said—"

"I know what your father thinks, but I'm the one who's sick, so I get the final word." My mother's voice grew sharper, some of the energy restored to her words. "I'm going to be doing my best. You have to do your best at camp. Promise me, Rui Na."

My throat was closing up, but I managed to choke out, "I—I promise, Mama."

"Rui Na?" Baba's face popped up close to the screen again. "Don't listen to your mother. It's your responsibility as our daughter to come back home now to be with your family. Do you hear me?"

"You shouldn't be discouraging Rui Na's dreams!" Mama shouted.

My mind was made up. "Baba—listen to me. I'm not going home." My voice shook, but I forced the words out before I could change my mind.

"What are you talking about?" Baba demanded.

I gulped, trying to stay strong. It was already too late to turn back. Opposing my father was scarier than facing down one hundred enemies in Dayhold—but I had to do it.

"I'm doing really well in this tournament. I'm enjoying my classes, too. Girls *can* game well. I'll show you. I'm going to win this tournament. Mama's right. We *both* have to do our best." At my words, Mama's smile widened, and I hoped—I *knew*—I'd made the right choice.

"Do whatever you want," my father said, and his voice sounded so detached and cold it frightened me. "But know that if you don't come home now, don't expect to come home, ever."

With a beep, he hung up the phone. I was left to listen to that horrible, horrible silence.

Shaking, I put the phone down. A small part of me, the obedient Reyna who'd always done her best to please both of her parents, screamed that I'd just made the worst mistake of my life.

But a bigger part of me, the Reyna who loved gaming and wanted to prove herself to the world, was even louder. That part of me said I'd done what was necessary.

I just hoped that part of me was right.

TEN

We had another day of break before the third round of the tournament. It was Liam's birthday, and a few days ago he'd invited Henry, Nell, and me to play games and eat cake with him in the commons area. As it turned out, he'd also invited a bunch of other kids, and even some of the upperclassmen—most I only vaguely recognized from class or in the hall.

Being around this many strangers was nerve-racking. I tried to enjoy the party but found I couldn't really get into the mood. In the back of my mind, I was constantly thinking about the explosive conversation I'd had with my parents. We hadn't spoken since last night. Every time I thought of my family, dread knotted my stomach.

And then, when I did manage to stop thinking about that awful fight, I still had the third round of the tournament to worry about.

". . . to Reyna? Hellooooooo. Is anyone in there?"

Someone was tapping my shoulder. I shook my head to clear it and had to take a moment to remember where I was: sitting on a big purple sofa in the commons room, surrounding by my classmates.

I turned and locked gazes with Nell, who was staring at me in concern. There was chocolate frosting smeared on his lips.

"You've got a little something here," I told him, pointing at the corner of my lips.

Looking embarrassed, Nell quickly swiped at the frosting with a napkin. "You good? You've been zoning out, like, all afternoon. And we're not even in Professor Kumar's class," he joked.

I let out a half-hearted laugh. "Yeah, I'm fine. Just feeling a little tired, is all." I was worried sick about Mama, and I wasn't close enough to anyone here to confide in them. I'd told Henry about Mama's surgery being on the same day as the tournament finals, but nobody else knew about what was going on in my family.

"Been staying up late watching the tournament?"

Playing in it, actually. "Yup. You?"

"Are you kidding me? Course I am! This is only the second tournament TheRuiNar has appeared in, ever. I've gotta cheer him on!"

Nell's enthusiasm brought the first smile to my face in what felt like days. "You should focus on your own gaming, doofus."

Nell rolled his eyes. "Hey, that goes for you, too. I've seen some of your moves in class."

"Me too," said Henry. "You're not bad, but you could use some improvement, Reyna."

Of course, they only knew my alt account, ReyningChamp, where I went out of my way to play decently but not *too* well. If only these guys knew my true skills.

"Attention, people!" Liam stood up on a leather lounge chair and clapped his hands together. Immediately, the ten-ish party-goers turned toward him. He adjusted his birthday hat, which had started to slip down his head. It had the number twelve on it. "Time for the main event of my birthday party: Dayhold freeplay!"

"Wait, what?" shouted a girl named Bethany Lewis. "Here? Now?"

"I don't have my gamer suit," complained Mimi.

"Are we livestreaming? I'm not ready!" cried Sanjeet,

frantically patting down his curly brown hair. "Does anyone have a mirror?"

Liam sighed. "Calm down, guys. We're just going to play the Pitch version of Dayhold." He squinted at the crowd of partygoers and pointed at us each in turn, as though counting heads. "There are eleven of us total, and I've borrowed ten Pitches from the community center, so I guess one of us will have to sit out."

"I'll sit out." An upperclassman guy I didn't recognize raised his hand.

"Perfect! All right. Let's do this. Hope you losers are ready to go down," Liam cackled.

"Please, Liam, I could beat you blindfolded with one arm tied behind my back," shouted Mimi, causing uproarious laughter. Liam frowned at her at first, but then even he joined in on the laughter, too.

"As if you could beat Liam," scoffed a blue-eyed upperclassman. I recognized him as one of the guys I'd seen trail Felix around school. "You're a girl."

Mimi bristled. At the boy's words, a pounding developed in my ears, and I felt my heartbeat quicken in anger.

"What's your point?" Mimi said frostily, though the tone

of her voice told us all that she knew *exactly* what the boy's point was.

"Um, Francis." Liam coughed. He motioned for the boy to stop talking, but Francis either didn't notice or didn't care.

"Everyone knows guys are better gamers than girls," Francis said with a nasty smirk. "Isn't that right, boys?"

He looked around for support. The tension in the air was so thick, I could almost see it. A few of the guys nodded, including Henry. I shot him a death glare, and he stopped.

"Yeah, uh, that's sexist and wrong," Mimi said flatly, and I immediately felt a rush of kinship for the other girl. Francis flushed. "We're just as good gamers as you are. Maybe even better."

"Better?" Francis snorted. "In your dreams."

"Why don't we prove it with a game of Dayhold, then?" I said, raising my Pitch controller. Somehow, I was keeping control of my temper. My parents would've been proud. "We'll see if girls make good gamers."

"You're on," said Francis.

I had to wipe that sneer off his face if it was the last thing I ever did. The stiffness in Mimi's shoulders and her determined expression told me she felt the same. We put up with these insults all the time. Enough. It was time to prove that girl gamers were every bit as capable—if not more—than boy gamers.

With a nervous laugh, Liam tried to cut through the thick tension in the air. "H-hey, guys, let's relax a little and have fun, okay? It's my ... my birthday ..." His voice faltered when he realized we were all but ignoring him.

Everyone took a Pitch and set up our systems so that we were all on the same network for the battlefield, which was projected onto the big screen in the community center. Since we could register with whatever username we wanted, I chose M00nshineNo1Fan.

"Good choice," Henry said approvingly. "M00nshine's the coolest."

I shot him a grin. "I know. She's one of my heroes."

With all the noise we'd been making, we'd drawn a crowd. Even some of the popular kids, including Felix and his friends, had stopped by to see what was happening. Pressure was *on*.

As it turned out, after all his boasting, Liam was knocked out of the game within five minutes. "What? No fair! I wasn't ready. Let's start over," he said.

"Sorry, Dayhold rules don't make exceptions, not even for the birthday boy," said Mimi smugly.

Soon, Francis threw his Pitch down in frustration, too. I had just thrown a bomb at him, destroying him instantly. Finally, the last two standing were Mimi and me, our avatars locked in a heated battle. Adrenaline soared in my blood, and in the heat of the moment, I'd even forgotten Francis's words and why I'd been so worked up in the first place.

With a well-timed blow of my sword, I struck down Mimi's avatar.

"Whoa, you're really good," Nell said, his voice over my shoulder startling me. I hadn't realized he'd crept so close. "I haven't seen you play like *this* before!"

"Oh man! I'm out. You win, Reyna," Mimi groaned a second later, sighing and setting her Pitch down. She wiped sweat off her forehead and then shot a self-satisfied smile around at all the boys. "So what was that about girls not being good gamers?"

The boys squirmed uncomfortably. Finally, some nervous laughter broke out, and after a few moments, the tension began to leave the room.

"Let's play again!" Liam shouted. "New rule: Nobody is allowed to attack the birthday boy."

"You goober, you just want to win," groaned Henry, rolling his eyes. Everyone laughed.

For the first time in a long time, I was actually having fun playing Dayhold. There was no stress in playing a casual game at Liam's birthday party. No $10,000 grand prize on the line. And I didn't have to worry about being TheRuiNar, rising star. I could just play for fun without the pressure of being TheRuiNar and winning. No pretending I wasn't as skilled. It was the most freeing, wonderful feeling in the world.

"Whoa! Reyna, how'd you do that?"

I blinked, as though coming out of a trance. Nell was staring at the replay on the screen, where my avatar had just feigned defeat and then taken down Henry's. Nell turned his eyes toward me. The only word to describe the expression on his face would be "awestruck." "You played like TheRuiNar. Drew in the opponent and pretended to be cornered, and then uppercut them. *Pow!*" Nell made an uppercut motion, nearly whacking Sanjeet, who dove out of the way. "Just like that. Just like how Professor Lucien taught us in Intermediate Strategy the other day."

"Oh. Um." Oh no. No no no. My heart thudded to a stop in my chest.

I hadn't realized Nell or anyone had been watching my game-play in the tournament so closely that they'd notice me pulling off similar moves now. I'd been having so much fun, I'd slipped up and forgotten to keep anything that might reveal me to be TheRuiNar strictly under wraps. And other people had been watching, too. Had they seen? Had they made the connection between TheRuiNar and me, like Nell had?

I was a terrible liar, but I had to try to worm my way out of this.

"I mean . . . I— Are—are you sure that's what you saw, Nell?" I stammered.

"I *know* what I saw," Nell insisted. "Wait. Reyna, does this mean you're . . . ?"

At Nell's words, Henry threw me a curious gaze. A few of the closest students perked up and looked at me, too.

Uh-oh. Panic seized me. I was in serious trouble. If Nell knew my identity as TheRuiNar, he would tell people. And there's no knowing what they'd say and do. Suddenly, horrible scenarios began running through my mind. Would Henry still be my best friend? Would I still be able to compete in the tournament? I pictured F3lx gloating to me that he *had* been cheating all along, before going on to win the $10,000 that should've been mine.

"Nell, it's not what you th—"

"Does this mean you're training to play like TheRuiNar?" Nell yelped in excitement, drawing stares from Liam's friends.

The sigh of relief I gave probably could've been heard at the other end of the school. Nell hadn't figured out who I was. He simply thought that I was a rabid fangirl. Which I guess was close enough to the truth. "Oh, um, yeah. Just, um, trying to play as well as TheRuiNar."

Henry gave me a funny look. I plastered my face with what I hoped was a totally innocent "I'm not TheRuiNar" expression. "Wait, really? I've never seen you play like this before. You're not usually . . . well, this good. No offense."

I shrugged, trying to play it off cool, even though I was panicking on the inside. "I've, uh, been studying TheRuiNar's moves."

"You should've told me this before, Reyna!" Nell said, looking annoyed. "We could've studied together. You know how much I like TheRuiNar. Hey, wanna give me a hand on making merch for him? It's a lot to handle for one guy . . ."

As Nell continued gushing about TheRuiNar, everyone else

shrugged and turned away from us. I heaved another sigh of relief. That had been a close one. Although I was pretty sure I hadn't been in any real danger of being doxed. Who would believe that one of the top prospects in the Junior Dayhold Tournament was a silver-level student, and a Chinese American girl, at that?

After Liam's birthday party, I headed back to my dorm to relax for the rest of the evening and get a full night of sleep. I needed all my energy for tomorrow.

I flopped onto my bed and automatically turned on the monitor to call home but then stopped myself.

Baba and I had had that awful fight last night. And we hadn't made up. And my parents hadn't called me since. My mood soured as I recalled the horrible things my father and I had said to each other, and I struggled to hold back tears.

Don't think about that now, I ordered myself. *Just focus on tomorrow's game.* No matter what kind of mess my family life was in, I couldn't let that affect my gameplay. If I lost the tournament now, I'd lose everything—my family, and my dream.

I turned the monitor off and lay flat on my back on my bed,

staring up at the ceiling. Suddenly, my room, which had always felt like the perfect size, seemed too big for one small gamer.

A notification popped up on my monitor screen, surprising me so much I almost fell off my bed.

You have one unread message.

When I opened the message, I thought it was a last-minute reminder of the rules for tomorrow's team round. But as I read it over, I quickly realized this was *definitely* not that.

Reyna Cheng:
You don't know me, but I know you. I know you're TheRuiNar. And if you don't withdraw from the tournament before the final round, I'll dox you. I can do that without even exposing my own identity.
Don't bother trying to track down the source of this message. Nothing you've learned in school can help you get out of this. And you'll never find out who I am, so don't even try.
You have 3 days. Withdraw, or else.

ELEVEN

I barely had time to read the threatening message through twice before it vanished from my inbox. With shaking hands, I clicked the refresh icon over and over again. But every time, my email came up empty. Had I just imagined the whole thing?

But no. There was no way I'd dream up something so awful. Even *my* imagination wasn't that wild.

Nothing you've learned at school can get you out of this. That made it sound like someone at school was threatening to dox me.

Someone at Dayhold Academy had found out my true identity.

Sweating, shivering, I lay back in bed, stunned. I'd been so careful about keeping my identity hidden. Who could have discovered the truth? Who could have sent a message threatening to dox me? If someone leaked my information, they could find my home. They could harass Mama, Baba, and me. Or *worse*.

My mind turned immediately to Nell, the only person who I'd ever even suspected of guessing that I was TheRuiNar. I dismissed the thought as quickly as it formed. No. Not Nell. Yes, he'd made the connection between TheRuiNar's gameplay and the way I'd played at Liam's birthday party—that was *super* careless of me—but he only thought I'd been copying TheRuiNar out of admiration. Plus, Nell was way too sweet to go around doxing people. And I'm pretty sure he didn't even have the time for that, since all his free time was dedicated to fanboying over TheRuiNar.

But it was too much of a coincidence that the doxer had sent their threatening message right after Liam's birthday party. It was the most likely scenario that that's where the mysterious messenger had figured out my identity. A whole group of Liam's friends, and plenty of strangers, had seen me do my specialty move. Any one of them could have guessed—correctly—that I was TheRuiNar.

I couldn't just sit here, spinning my wheels in the dirt as I tried to put together what had happened this afternoon. I needed answers. And I was pretty sure I could get at least a couple of them from one person.

Flinging my door open, I rushed out into the hall. I had twenty minutes until lights-out, when Mr. Porter would come punishing any students for being out of bed. I had to do something important before then.

There was a curly-haired boy standing outside a nearby room, who I vaguely recognized as Justin Tran from my Advanced Combat class, glancing at me with a startled expression on his face. I was probably wild-eyed and looked every bit of the mess that I felt on the inside, but I didn't care.

"Hey, do you know where Liam Russ's room is?" I asked.

"Oh, um ... make a left turn down this hall, and he's the third door on your left," Justin said, pointing down the hall. He looked mystified.

"Great. Thanks." I sped past him and made a beeline for Liam's room. When I reached the third door on my left, I knocked on it. "Liam? Liam!"

"Coming," came the muffled response. I waited impatiently, and some shuffling noises came from inside. A moment later, the door swung open, and Liam stood there in his pajamas. His hair was mussed up on one side, like he'd slept sideways. "Oh, hey, Reyna. What's up?"

"Um . . ." This was going to be a strange conversation no matter what. Resigning myself to that fact, I continued, "This might sound like a weird question, but I promise I wouldn't be asking if it weren't *really* important."

Liam shrugged. "Shoot."

"Can you give me the names of everyone who went to your birthday party?"

He blinked at me, the surprise evident on his face. "Uh . . . everyone who went to my birthday party? Why do you want to know?" His eyebrows drew together. "Did something happen?"

"Yeah . . . I mean, no. Sorta?"

He leaned against the doorframe, studying me with narrowed eyes. "You're acting weird, Reyna. Weirder than normal."

"Wow. Thanks."

"What's going on?"

I bit my lip. There was no way I could tell Liam I was in danger of being doxed. Revealing that was as good as telling him that I was a semifinalist in the tournament. "I'll explain everything later," I said hastily, even though I was pretty sure I wouldn't. "Just trust me, it's really important. Can you just tell me who was at your party?"

After giving me another long look, Liam shrugged. "Wish I could, but *I* don't even know who came."

"Huh? What do you mean?"

"I only invited you and a few of our classmates—Nell, Henry, Mimi, and Sanjeet. I have no idea who invited those upperclassmen who showed up with Felix. They were pretty cool, though." He wrinkled his nose. "Except Francis. He was kind of a jerk."

My shoulders slumped. Great. So Liam himself didn't even know who half the partygoers were. I was pretty sure that none of my classmates would dox me, either. At least, I really wanted to believe they wouldn't.

I opened my mouth to press Liam for more information, but the strange look he gave me made me hesitate. The last thing I wanted was to attract *any* suspicion.

"Okay, well, thanks, anyway," I said, forcing some fake cheer into my voice.

"Why do you sound like a dying mule?"

I dropped the fake cheeriness. "I do *not*."

Liam grinned. "That sounds more like you."

"Good night, Liam," I huffed. Then after a moment I added, "Oh, and happy birthday."

"Thanks," Liam said. "Next year, though, I don't want cake. I just want y'all to go easy on me and let me win a round of Dayhold freeplay for once, okay?"

I rolled my eyes. "Okay, okay."

"You should get back to your room. Lights-out is in five minutes."

After Liam and I said good night, I fast-walked down the hall before Mr. Porter could come prowling around. As I slipped into my room just before ten o'clock p.m., a thought struck me.

Next year, Liam had said, as though it were a given that we'd all be back at camp to celebrate his birthday again. He didn't know it, but my scholarship only covered this summer.

And now, thanks to this anon, I didn't even know if I could last the last couple weeks of it.

The next day, I woke up feeling less than refreshed for the third round of the Junior Dayhold Tournament. The mystery of that message had kept me up way too late, and through the whole day into the late afternoon, I still couldn't stop thinking about it.

My usual pregame ritual of singing and dancing to K-pop failed to energize me today. Thanks to a combination of tournament fatigue, lack of sleep, balancing my schoolwork and alt account, and stress over my secret being found out, I was running on empty. I had a feeling that even the worst player at the academy could give me a thrashing. Forget being doxed. I was about to lose fair and square.

"No! You can't think like that, Reyna. Focus. Eyes on the prize," I scolded myself, slapping both of my cheeks. The sting was painful, but at least it helped wake me up.

This was an evening that called for some extra help. I ordered a pot of coffee along with a lox bagel. Baba and Mama had never let me drink coffee when I was at home, claiming that it wasn't good for a growing kid's body, but here, there were no adults to boss me around.

Soon, my tray arrived. I poured myself a huge, piping-hot mug of room-service coffee and dumped as much milk and sugar as I wanted into it. This was going to be delicious. I took a big sip and choked. "Blech! That's *way* too sugary."

My holographic screen turned on as I was dumping the mug of coffee into the bathroom sink. I rushed back just in time to see Commander Dayhold's face appear on the screen. He was going over the rules of today's round, and I didn't want to miss anything.

"Evening, Dayholders!" exclaimed the commander.

Something told me Commander Dayhold probably had a huge cup of coffee every hour. How else would the guy have so much energy whenever he spoke to us?

"The third round of the Junior Dayhold Tournament takes place in half an hour," the commander continued. "Most of the rules remain the same as the previous rounds, but there will be a slight difference for the semifinals. This is a team round, with each of the remaining twenty-five gamers split into five teams of five. You won't find out who's on your team until you've entered the gaming arena, but it'll be obvious once you do so—you'll each be wearing the same color armband, except for the team captain of each group, whose armband will also have a 'C.' Your focus will be on taking down opponents and scoring as many points as possible for your team. Three hundred points will be awarded with the elimination of each player on the opposing teams, and five hundred points for the elimination of the opposing teams' leaders. At the end of the time limit—one hour—the team with the most earned points will advance to the final round, where those five remaining players will battle it out to determine the runner-up and champion."

Teamwork. I'd always hated teamwork in school, because it seemed like one person—aka *me*—got saddled with all the work, while everyone else could slack off.

I sighed, thinking back to the past two rounds of the tournament, where I'd struck secret alliances with other members. Yeah, that hadn't turned out so well in the end. But this time, all the gamers would be working in teams, whether we wanted to or not. At least that meant nobody could try to backstab each other, since that'd be self-sabotage.

At least there was a time limit of one hour for the semifinals, though. It was a relief to know that in sixty minutes, it would all be over.

After changing into my gamer suit—the baby-pink one this time—and putting on my gloves, I did my best to pump myself up for the game. But it was hard to get excited. My stomach churned with nerves. There was a lot riding on this competition. I'd come so far already. If I got eliminated now, *this* close to winning the tournament, it would be devastating.

Plus, there was the very real chance that one of the gamers

would dox me. In the letter, the person had said they'd dox me if I didn't drop out before the final round, but what if they changed their mind and decided to do it earlier?

I couldn't let that happen. Not in this round, and not in the final round. That meant I had two tasks for the semifinals. One: Make sure my team made it to the finals. And two: Figure out who was trying to dox me—and silence them somehow.

"Here goes nothing," I said as I stepped up to the screen, all suited up. With a flash, I was transported to the stage of the third round of the Junior Dayhold Tournament.

TWELVE

The third round brought us back to the magical setting of the WeiXian Forest from qualifiers. After I landed on the hard, dirt-packed floor, I straightened and quickly adjusted to my surroundings. It was a reflex at this point. The forest at night was dark and cold, with only fireflies to illuminate the path. The virtual world was still, with not even a whisper of wind disturbing the atmosphere. It was deceptively peaceful.

One glance showed me who my teammates were to be. Four gamers dusted themselves off around me. For a long moment, nobody said anything as we sized each other up.

In game, our suits had all transformed to the same matching vibrant orange color. Additionally, red armbands had appeared around my teammates' left arms. When I looked down at my arm,

I discovered I had one, too—but it had a "C." Which meant ... somehow, *I'd* been chosen to be the team leader.

I gulped. I had no idea how to run a team. But even if these gamers would never listen to little Reyna in real life, they'd listen to the fierce and confident TheRuiNar in Dayhold.

I looked around at the speech bubbles above the gamers' heads, which told me their usernames.

Amefyst. Drag0n. Dustin955.

And ... F3lx.

For a long beat, the five of us just stood there. I'd heard of all these players before and knew they had to be pretty good since they'd made it to the third round. But it was F3lx who really caught my interest. All the rumors about his gameplay traveled around the scene. Plus, he'd basically declared war against me in the last round.

At first, I was annoyed that he was on my team, but then it occurred to me that this scenario couldn't have worked out better for me. What was that saying—keep your friends close, and your enemies closer? With F3lx right under my nose, I could watch him closely to see if he really was as good as the rumors said. To see if he'd cheat.

Maybe I'd actually lucked out by having F3lx on my team.

DragOn raised an arm in a casual greeting.

DragOn: Yo. Looks like we're all on the same team, huh?

TheRuiNar: Looks like it.

Dustin955: Should we give ourselves a team name?

F3lx: Let's call ourselves The Winning Team.

We all stared at F3lx.

DragOn: Wow, someone's got confidence.

F3lx: What, do you think we're gonna lose?

Amefyst: I don't see why we even have to do this in teams. Dayhold was designed to be a single-player battle royale game.

TheRuiNar: They probably want a well-rounded champion— someone who can do individual and team battle.

Dustin955: Whatever, it doesn't matter. Let's just come up with a game plan, stat. We've only got an hour to destroy the other teams.

F3lx: One hour is plenty. In fact, if you guys want me to handle this, I could take them out on my own.

F3lx's constant bragging was getting on my last nerve, and judging by the reactions from the other three, I wasn't the only one he'd ticked off.

Amefyst: If you're so good, then why would you need us? Go on your own, then. No one's stopping you.

F3lx shrugged, readjusted the strap of his messenger bag, and turned around to leave, but I rushed to block his path. He tried to walk past me, but I flung out an arm to stop him.

F3lx: Problem, TheRuiNar?

I hated confrontation, but I could tell that unless we got everyone on the same page, we were all going to be easy targets for the other teams. And no matter what, I had to make sure I advanced to the next round.

When I spoke, I addressed all four of my teammates.

TheRuiNar: Guys, Commander Dayhold told us the rules this morning. And the rules are that we win this round as a team. It's only for one hour. Then after that—after we win and move on to finals—we can fight individually again. If you can't do something like this for an hour, then you don't deserve to call yourself a Dayhold champion, anyway.

I knew that what I'd said would ruffle their feathers. Gamers were so proud—to a fault. Especially gamers who were used to coming out on top.

Drag0n: He's right.

Amefyst: We should come up with a strategy.

F3lx didn't say anything, but he didn't walk away, either. I guess that meant my message had gotten through to him.

Dustin955: We don't have time for a complicated strategy. Don't need one, either. The rules are simple. All we gotta do is destroy the other teams.

TheRuiNar: Okay, well, we should at least agree on an attack pattern. Do we want to adopt a wait-and-see approach, or do we want to go out and attack?

The other gamers stared at each other, and then turned back to me.

Go out and attack, said their speech bubbles all at once.

No surprise there. I guess asking Dayholders to "wait and see" was pretty futile. We were attackers by nature, which was why we loved the battle royale format.

TheRuiNar: I think we have to be sneakier than that, since it's the finals. How about this—we can send out one or two team members as bait, and then the rest of us sneak up on the enemy teams when their attention is diverted. How many of you have cloaks?

Everyone except Drag0n raised their hands.

TheRuiNar: That's settled. Drag0n, you'll be the bait.

Drag0n: Oh boy . . .

TheRuiNar: Don't worry, I'll protect you. I'll charge up with you.

Amefyst: I'll protect ya, too, big guy.

Drag0n: Hey, who says I need protecting?!

TheRuiNar: Okay, back to the plan, though—everyone activate your cloaks so the enemy can't see you coming on their heat sensors. Drag0n and I will lead the charge toward enemy teams.

F3lx: What if other teams have the same plan?

TheRuiNar: Then we'll just have to outfight them in the battle.

Dustin955: Roger that!

TheRuiNar: Let's do this! Don't get eliminated. We're fighting creatures in the game, too—don't forget!

Right as I finished speaking, a hú li jīng charged at me out of nowhere. I sliced it in half with my trusty weapon, the Ruyi Jingu Bang. When the demon disintegrated, I looked up to find F3lx watching me. For some reason, that made me feel uneasy.

F3lx: Nice work.

TheRuiNar: Um . . . thanks.

"Plus fifty points," my Codex said as it took my demon kill into account. The bar in the corner of my helmet glowed and increased.

Everyone except Drag0n activated our cloaks. Our heat sources disappeared in my field of vision. We could still be seen and attacked by demons in the game, but not by other players—at least, not until we were right in front of them. Hopefully, this was enough to give us the element of surprise on our side.

As we charged through the forest, led by Drag0n and me, I kept an eye on the nearby heat sources and directed us toward the nearest cluster. My heart pounded with the electrifying excitement of running directly toward danger.

We encountered the first team, a group of five gamers wearing all black. They either didn't have cloaks or hadn't activated them, because all their heat sources were visible. As planned, Drag0n jumped on one of their players, and they both went tumbling into the road. I engaged the nearest player, but the gamer was quicker to react and leapt aside. Though the opposing gamers shouted in surprise, they regained their composure swiftly.

Four orange, four black. We circled each other, waiting for an excuse to launch into attack.

Before we engaged in combat, one of the gamers—his username bubble said NightRyder, who I recognized as another up-and-coming gamer—stepped forward. My eyes immediately were drawn to the black band with a "C" on it around his arm, which indicated that he'd been chosen to be this group's leader.

NightRyder: Who's your leader?

My teammates looked to me. I stepped forward.

TheRuiNar: That'd be me.

NightRyder pulled out his sword and pointed it at me. I stared

down the blade, proud that not even a muscle trembled.

NightRyder: Team, remind me. What's a captain's elimination
worth again?
RunsOnDunkin: Five hundred points.
NightRyder: Boys, watch and learn. This is how you earn five
hundred points in style.

I couldn't tell what it was exactly that irked me so much about
NightRyder. Maybe it was the way he called his whole team "boys."
Yet another reminder that girls were barely even acknowledged as
players in Dayhold. Maybe it was his cocky attitude.

Guess it was up to me to deliver NightRyder a much-needed
reality check.

TheRuiNar: Team—leave this jerk to me. Take care of the others.

Amefyst: Aye, aye, Captain.

Around me, the sound of swords clashing filled the air. NightRyder and I took slow, measured steps toward each other. Adrenaline thrummed through my body. I attacked first. Swinging the Ruyi Jingu Bang in an arc, I aimed for NightRyder's head. He dodged easily, and then caught me in the stomach with a round-house kick.

The force of the impact threw me back several feet, but I managed to keep my footing. *Focus*, I commanded myself. This wasn't a practice round. There was no room to make mistakes now. If I went down, the other team would have a huge points advantage.

When NightRyder charged at me, I brought up the shaft of my staff to block his attack. My teeth clenched together. My arm muscles trembled despite my suit softening the hit.

NightRyder: While I've got you here, I have a question for you, TheRuiNar.

He was acting so casual, like we were just two people having a pleasant conversation in the woods. This guy seriously was getting on my nerves. I gritted my teeth.

TheRuiNar: What is it?

NightRyder: Are you . . . a girl?

The shock of the question threw me off so much that my arms let up. NightRyder took advantage of the slight opening and shoved me back. I couldn't stop myself from losing my balance. My backside hit the ground, and pain shot down my body. My staff spun out of my hands and landed several feet away.

NightRyder: Yeah, only a girl player would pull a pathetic move like that.

Ignoring the pain pounding all over, I tried to leap to my feet to get to my Ruyi Jingu Bang, but NightRyder stomped down on my chest with his boots.

His persistency, his calling me a girl—maybe *NightRyder* was the person who'd threatened to dox me. I tried to connect his username with a real-world face, but unfortunately I had no clue who he was. He must be a player who was participating in the Junior Dayhold Tournament outside of our school.

NightRyder leaned down, and even though I couldn't see his face, I could picture the snarl on it.

NightRyder: What's the matter, no comebacks this time?

TheRuiNar: Leave me alone!

NightRyder: Huh? No can do. See, the point of this game is for me to destroy you.

All the jeering brought back horrible memories. I'd done my best to bury them, but now they sprang loose. Boys bullying me because I had my mic on and they could hear my voice. Boys calling me names, calling me weak because I was a girl. Boys chasing me out of Dayhold.

This time, I'd chosen to keep my identity hidden, my mic muted. But that hadn't changed things. Not really. Boys were still thinking "gamer girls" couldn't play, and someone—maybe NightRyder, or maybe someone else—had threatened to dox me.

I was sick of this.

NightRyder kicked my leg, and the jolt traveled up my body. He knew he had me cornered and weaponless. Now he was taking his sweet time before eliminating me, taunting me all the while.

NightRyder: I thought you'd be a tougher opponent. Everyone keeps talking about how you're supposed to be one of the best players. Some team leader you are.

Team leader. I twisted my gaze toward my red armband. I had a whole team depending on me to make it through this round.

This was no time to give up, no matter what stupid insults NightRyder or any other player dished out. I had to fight. If I got eliminated now, at least I'd go down fighting.

Without giving NightRyder a chance to react, I leapt up and caught him in the neck with a roundhouse kick. He shouted out in a mixture of surprise and pain. Using his back as a springboard, I leapt over to where my Ruyi Jingu Bang lay on the ground.

NightRyder was howling as he rolled on the ground, clutching his neck. I raised my staff high in the air.

TheRuiNar: Hope you've learned your lesson. Don't ever, ever mess with me.

I didn't hesitate to bring it down onto his body with a loud *crack!* He was still. A moment later, his body dissolved into thin air.

"Plus five hundred points," Codex said.

Even though I'd won the showdown and earned my team a slew of points, I felt no pleasure. Instead, there was only a sinking sensation in the pit of my stomach.

NightRyder's taunts had been annoying to endure, but I had no proof that he'd been the one who sent the email threat.

And if I didn't do something about that doxer—and soon—the situation was going to continue spiraling out of my control.

THIRTEEN

As the dust settled on the forest floor, I glanced around at my surroundings. The scene was a lot quieter now. Most of the players had disappeared—among them Amefyst, Drag0n, and Dustin955, I realized with a heavy heart. The only gamers left fighting were F3lx and two players on the other team, TRX23 and AdamSlays.

I rushed over to help F3lx fend off a relentless attack from TRX23. But I was still several feet too far away when AdamSlays aimed to stab F3lx right in the chest. F3lx's body spasmed, his avatar flickering, and then he began to fall.

"No!" I gasped.

F3lx couldn't get eliminated now. It was all over, especially if I was all on my own.

But then a miracle happened. I had to blink several times to make sure I was seeing things correctly.

TRX23 and AdamSlays, who had both homed in for the kill, stopped moving completely. For a few moments, it appeared as though they'd glitched. The scenario jarred a memory from my mind—in the last round, I'd frozen for a moment, too. Were these just bugs in the game?

Those precious few seconds were all F3lx needed to turn the situation on its head. Mid-fall, he placed a hand on the ground. His avatar stopped flickering and turned fully solid once more. Using his arm as balance, he kicked his feet up into the air.

Whack. Thud.

F3lx connected solidly with the two frozen gamers' chins, sending them flying backward. Then he straightened and started after the fallen gamers.

I raced forward, shoving F3lx back.

F3lx: What the heck?

TheRuiNar: You're injured. Eat a healing peach, and stay back. I'll take care of these guys!

I reached into my bag for three materials: Wire. Fuse. Gunpowder.

On the ground, the gamers were stirring, no longer frozen. Before AdamSlays could get to his feet, I slammed him away by catching him in the stomach with the end of my Ruyi Jingu Bang.

AdamSlays went down again. And this time, he wasn't coming back up. I was making sure of it.

TRX23 had already stood up and charged toward F3lx, but he didn't make it far. I brought the bomb out of my bag and tossed it at him and AdamSlays.

TheRuiNar: DUCK, F3LX!

As fast as my legs would carry me, I raced for cover in a cluster of bushes. I closed my eyes and shielded my Codex by throwing my arms over my head.

BOOM!

The earth rocked beneath my feet. The vibrations from the explosion lasted for maybe thirty seconds before subsiding. When the earth was steady again, I emerged from the bushes. Red and black dust—all that was left of the two gamers and the trees that had been there before—floated in the air above the scorched dirt.

F3lx stood up and walked over to me. He stopped. For a moment, neither of us said anything. Then:

F3lx: You could've let me handle those two guys. I didn't need you to butt in.

I rolled my eyes, before remembering he couldn't see it. Did this guy know how to say "thank you"?

TheRuiNar: Yeah, because you were handling it sooo well before I saved you.

F3lx: Well, I *was* handling the situation. I had everything under control. You just wanted to show off.

TheRuiNar: Show off? I saved your butt, you ungrateful—

"Plus three hundred points. Plus three hundred points," my Codex interrupted, flashing red in my vision.

F3lx and I stared at each other.

TheRuiNar: *Whoa.* That's six hundred more points.

F3lx: Yeah, for a total of . . . two thousand one hundred points.

Commander Dayhold's voice came over the helmet. "And with that explosive ending—literally—we've come to the end of the third round of the Junior Dayhold Tournament. Viewers, I present to you your winning team and tournament *finalists*: F3lx! Amefyst! Drag0n! Dustin955! Aaaaaaand, TheRuiNar! Congratulations, you five!"

As the commander shouted each of their names, Amefyst, Drag0n, and Dustin955 reappeared in front of us.

Amefyst was the first to recover and gave us all a cool nod.

Amefyst: Sup, finalists?

Drag0n: Don't "sup" us. It's your fault we were both eliminated this round. We could've lost because of you!

Amefyst: My fault? Whose idea was it to try to take down those two gamers 'cause they "looked weak"? They totally kicked our butts . . .

As the two continued to argue, a pounding headache developed over my right eye. It was a miracle that the five of us had managed to work together long enough to actually win this round, without strangling each other in the process. Also, in the heat of battle, I had hardly given a second thought to my other task— tracking down the person who'd threatened me.

Dustin955: Okay, that's enough! Amefyst, Drag0n, if you guys want to settle this fight, you can do that in two days during finals.

Amefyst: Oh, it's *on* during finals.

Drag0n: Yeah, this was fun and all, but there can only be one winner, and it's gonna be me.

F3lx: Big talk for someone who didn't make it to the end of the round.

"I see you Dayholders still have plenty of energy," chuckled Commander Dayhold's voice in our helmets. "Good, good. You've done well to make it this far. But there can only be one champion. Forty-six hours from now, we'll head into the fourth and final round of the tournament. Once the winner has been decided, there will be a closing ceremony, where you will reveal your identities to the Fuzion team—and the world."

I froze. *We would do what?*

"Rest as much as you can. You'll need it."

The next day was Saturday. It was another break day in the tournament schedule, so I had a ton of free time. Henry and Nell invited me to go Rollerblading in the park, but I turned them down with the excuse that I was feeling under the weather.

It wasn't a total lie. I was utterly drained from fighting round after round in the tournament. Plus, I was beyond stressed. The tournament guidelines had never mentioned revealing ourselves to thousands of viewers.

I wasn't in the mood for doing anything fun, not even hanging out with my friends.

Before I left, Henry pulled me aside. "You don't look so good," he told me flatly. "You look like something the cat dragged in, to be honest."

"Thanks, Henry." At least I could always count on my best friend to be honest with me.

"Okay, but really, I'm worried. Are you sick?"

I shook my head, averting my eyes so Henry couldn't read the truth on my face. I was sure my expression was screaming "TIRED

OF HIDING A MILLION SECRETS." "No, just having trouble sleeping." It wasn't a lie. Between battling nonstop, dodging sexist comments, and hiding my true identity, I couldn't remember the last time I'd gotten a good night of sleep. It didn't help that Mama was about to undergo surgery, and Baba was still upset with me choosing to stay at the academy.

"Is this about your mom's surgery?" Henry asked, his eyes bright with concern.

I swallowed and nodded. "Yeah."

"You *are* doing the right thing by staying at camp," Henry said. "I mean, you said even your mom told you to stay. So stop worrying so much, okay?"

"I'll try." Though I was pretty certain there was no way I could stop worrying, with so many concerns piling onto my plate.

Not only did I have to deal with someone threatening me, but now I had to prepare to show the whole Dayhold world who I was? At least I hadn't gotten any more messages. NightRyder might've been the culprit, but I wasn't sure. It could be anyone. The doxer had given me until the final round of the tournament to back out, after all. This wasn't over. I had to keep my guard up, until I caught whoever was behind that threat. My stomach twisted in fear.

I thought about Liam's birthday party. Even if Liam didn't know exactly who had attended, I could conjure some details about the partygoers. Like the fact that they were mostly guys. And mostly kids of color. That didn't give me much to go off of, but it was still a start.

Or—if Liam couldn't give me any solid clues, maybe the system itself could. There had to be a way to trace emails that entered my inbox, even if that particular message had vanished after I opened it. Maybe one of my professors would know. Maybe one of them could help me retrieve the message, pinpoint its origin.

I left my room and set off down the hall at a fast pace. I hoped at least one of my professors was still somewhere at school, in their classroom or wandering these halls. I spotted a few students here and there, stragglers heading back to their rooms, but no professors in sight. I approached the Dayhold Hall of Fame—and there, coming right out of that hall, was Professor Nakamura, my Gaming Nutrition professor.

"Professor!"

He turned toward me, fixing me with his sharp black eyes, and gave me a small smile. "Reyna."

"Professor, I—I have to ask you something. It's...kind of a weird question."

"Weird questions are the best kind of questions," said Professor Nakamura. "What is it?"

"Um..." I lowered my voice and looked around to make sure nobody could overhear us, even though there was no one in sight. "How possible would it be for someone to, like...hack into an email?"

Professor Nakamura blinked. Clearly, whatever "weird question" he'd been expecting, that hadn't been one of them. "Hack? Someone tried to hack your account?"

"No, someone sent me a—a weird email. I clicked it to read the message, but it disappeared, and I haven't been able to retrieve it since."

"You checked your trash folder? Your other files, too?"

"Yeah," I said impatiently. Did Professor Nakamura really think I would be panicking through these halls if I hadn't checked every nook and cranny for the mysterious message? "I haven't misplaced it. It just vanished."

"That's strange. If you don't mind me asking, what was in the contents of the email?"

I flushed, dropping my gaze to my feet. I couldn't help but feel guilty about what I was hiding, even though there was no way my professor could know. "I . . . um, it's a secret. Nothing bad," I rushed to clarify. "Just something I'd rather the other students don't find out."

"I understand."

Relief flooded me. I glanced back up to meet Professor Nakamura's kind gaze.

"But unfortunately, I've never heard of emails vanishing without a trace, and I'm in serious doubt that any other teachers would know what to do about that, either. The academy is up to date with the world's best technology, so it would have to have been the work of a very, very skilled hacker—someone with backdoor knowledge." Professor Nakamura's thoughtful expression turned skeptical. "Are you sure you didn't mistake this email for something else? Maybe check your spam or trash folder one more time?"

The relief became frustration. My professor didn't believe me. Of course he didn't. I wouldn't believe me, either. Why would someone with the power to hack into state-of-the-art technology use it to threaten me, and not do something . . . bigger? The more

I thought about it, the more far-fetched my story sounded even to me.

"Um, one more question," I said, playing the last card I had in my hand. "Is there a student here whose username is NightRyder?"

Professor Nakamura arched an eyebrow. "NightRyder? You mean the gamer who got eliminated in the latest round of the Junior Dayhold Tournament?"

I nodded. "Only asking because, um, I was really impressed by NightRyder's gameplay."

"I'm afraid I don't know, Reyna. That player must be entering the tournament from outside the school."

There went my last shred of hope. Trying not to look too disappointed, I said, "Thank you, Professor. I ... I'll check my inbox again." I didn't wait for the professor's response before turning on my heel and leaving.

FOURTEEN

In my room, I paced back and forth. I'd checked all my email folders once again. No trace of the mysterious email.

I was so wrapped up in my own thoughts, I almost didn't hear the *ping!* of an email landing in my inbox.

It's them, I thought, heart hammering.

When I pulled up the email, expecting to see another threat, I was quickly surprised. It wasn't the doxer. This email had the official Dayhold logo, which was the word "Dayhold" in white all-caps letters and red-orange flames behind it. Directly below it were the words *Junior Dayhold Tournament Finals: Admit One.*

A ticket to the finals! I scanned the body of the email, which explained that each of the five finalists received one free ticket to invite a friend or family member to watch the final round in the Dayhold stadium.

Who could I bring? Baba? I shook off the thought. My father and I hadn't said a word to each other since we'd fought the other night. He hadn't called me. I hadn't called him. I couldn't exactly call home now and ask Baba to come watch me in the finals, could I?

I sat down on my bed and drew my knees up to my chest, suddenly feeling very small in the huge bed. My eyes rose until they landed on my posters of LuckyJade847 and M00nshine. What would my idols do if they were in my shoes?

Follow your heart, LuckyJade847 always liked to say in her interviews. She definitely would've given me the same advice, if she were here to talk to me.

I squeezed my eyes shut. If I listened to my heart, I already knew what I wanted to do. The answer was clear.

Swallowing the last of my pride, I dialed home on my phone. It clicked on the third ring.

"Hello?"

"Baba?"

Silence.

"Rui Na?"

It was hard to interpret my father's tone over a voice call. But he didn't sound particularly emotional. Not that he ever did, even in person. I was just glad that he'd picked up my call. That had to mean that he wasn't still so angry that he didn't want me to be his daughter anymore. Right?

"H-how's Mama?"

"Still at the hospital. Her condition has stabilized, and she's preparing for the operation."

I let out a breath of relief. Hearing this news made my heart feel instantly fifty pounds lighter. Though I was upset that nobody had told me the news earlier. "That's good," I said. When Baba was silent, I added worriedly, "Isn't it?"

"Yes, it's good. But your mother is about to go into surgery. She's not in the clear yet."

Another long, painful silence. I shuffled my feet. "Um . . . so listen, Baba. I . . . I made it to the finals of the Junior Dayhold Tournament."

"Oh." A pause. "Congratulations."

Hearing that one word of praise from my father was enough to take the air out of my lungs for a moment. "You . . . you mean it?"

"Gaming isn't very suitable for young girls, but not many play-ers, boys or girls, can make it to the finals," my father rattled off, almost like he'd prepared those words ahead of time. Almost like someone more favorable to the e-sport—*Mama*—had talked some sense into him.

I blinked back tears. Now was *not* the time to get all sappy! "So, um, the reason I called is . . . is because the finals are happening tomorrow. They gave me a ticket. I . . . I wanted to ask if you'd come watch. If you'd like to, that is. And if you're free. I can message the ticket to you." The words tumbled out in my nerves. Once Baba looked for me among the competitors, he'd know I was TheRuiNar. He'd know I'd been gaming under a totally different username, that I'd hidden the truth from him and Mama. But I knew, too, that I wanted to come clean to my parents. To show them who I really was, and what I was capable of doing.

This time, the silence that greeted me felt longer and emptier than all the past silences combined. Holding my breath, I waited for Baba's answer.

"Rui Na, this is very sudden. I don't think I can take the time off work. And then there's the matter of your mother's surgery, too. My schedule is too full."

"Oh." My shoulders drooped. I'd prepared for this response, but it didn't make it any less disappointing. *My schedule is too full—for you.* That's what it sounded like. "That's okay. It is pretty last minute. I'll forward you the email, though, anyway."

It couldn't be helped, after all. I'd asked Baba with less than a day's notice. Of course he couldn't just skip work to come to a Dayhold tournament.

"Good luck on the finals, Rui Na," Baba said. "You'll come home soon after that, right?"

"Yeah. The camp will be almost over then." A pang entered my chest at the thought. I didn't want to leave behind Dayhold Academy. I wanted to keep learning from the greatest instructors and be the best player I could be. Playing Dayhold felt like . . . my life's calling. I knew that I was still super young to be thinking stuff like that already, but the deepest part of my core was absolutely, 100 percent certain. From the moment I'd first begun playing the game, I knew I was meant for this. Meant to play Dayhold.

I wanted to say all these things to my father, but the words wouldn't come out. What was the point? He would never understand. To him, the point of a career was to earn stable money, not to chase your dreams. Dreams were for the rich, the privileged. Not for immigrants or their children.

"Bye, Baba," I said instead.

"Goodbye."

After my father and I hung up, I went back to staring at my posters for a long, long time. Thinking about finals tomorrow. Thinking about how M00nshine and LuckyJade847 had proudly worn their labels as girl gamers. Thinking about how I was going to outsmart an invisible enemy.

I thought for so long that the sun dipped in the sky, and dinnertime came and went before I realized it. Finally, I realized that with so little time until the finals, no leads on the doxer's identity, and the commander's heads-up about the ceremony, there was no way to win against this doxer.

When I couldn't stand the deafening silence any longer, I got up and went for a walk through the commons area to stretch my legs. Since most of our coursework was done now, all the underclassmen were lounging around or going outside to enjoy what remained of summer.

"Hey, Reyna!"

At the sound of my name, I turned around. Henry and Nell

were both sitting on the couch, eating Dayhold-themed fruit snacks and waving at me. The sight of my friends lifted my spirits considerably.

"Hey," I said, sitting down and swiping a bag of fruit snacks from the community bowl.

"I was just about to come find you," Nell said eagerly. He reached into his pocket and yanked out a slip of paper, thrusting it in my face.

"Whoa!" I lurched away, rubbing my nose. "You almost gave me a paper cut."

"Oh. Sorry. But look at it! My ticket to the Junior Dayhold Tournament finals came today," Nell exclaimed. "And I hear that at the end, they'll be revealing all the finalists' identities so the pros can scout them more easily." He sighed and leaned back against the couch, staring up at the ceiling with a dreamy look on his face. "Boy, I can't *wait* to discover who TheRuiNar is. I bet he's someone real strong and powerful, with huge muscles!"

I stared down at my scrawny chicken arms and stick-thin legs, a knot forming in my stomach. Looked like Nell was in for a real disappointment tomorrow.

"Reyna, are you okay? You don't... look so good," said Nell, studying my face.

"No, I'm fine." I forced a smile, even though I kind of wanted to throw up. Somehow, until this moment, I hadn't really considered what it meant that Henry, Nell, and all my friends and classmates and teachers were going to be watching me from the audience for the final round of the tournament. And that felt a whole lot different than knowing they were watching from a livestream from their bedrooms. A whole lot scarier.

"I got my ticket today, too," Henry said excitedly. "Man, it really feels like the summer camp is winding down now, right? What're you guys gonna do after this? My mom and pops got lucky with their investments this year, so we've got extra money. They're letting me enroll in Dayhold Academy for the school year!"

Nell and I gaped at Henry in open envy. "Whoa, Henry. You're so lucky," Nell sighed. He wrinkled his nose. "Me, I'm going back to public school. My parents can't afford to send me to the academy year-round. But I'll *definitely* be back for summer camp next year."

"I don't know if I'll be able to come back next summer," I

admitted, "but Henry and I live pretty close, in Brooklyn, so we'll still be able to hang out and stuff. And you guys have my video chat ID and we can always play games together whenever you want."

"Anytime, anywhere," Henry reassured me.

"Count me in. I'm always ready to beat you guys," said Nell.

We laughed. For the first time in ages, I felt a sense of calm—but only for a moment. All the problems of real life, Mama's surgery and the finals, snapped me back to reality. I headed back to my room to relax, but then another message notification popped up onto my monitor screen, and I knew who it was from even before I opened it.

If you don't back out of tomorrow's finals, you'll regret it. I already know where you live. Are you ready to lose in front of the whole world—and for everyone to find out who you are?

I went to take a screenshot, but once again, the email vanished before I could do anything. I bit my lip in frustration. Anger boiled inside me. Who was this person? Had they really found my address? My doubts that NightRyder was the doxer were confirmed by this email. *Are you ready to lose in front of the whole world?* It sounded like the true culprit was going to be playing in the finals tomorrow. Maybe I was reading too much into the wording, but my gut told me I wasn't.

This gamer thought they had me cornered, hiding behind their computer screen and hacking into the system, but they had no idea how wrong they were. It didn't matter if I couldn't track down this coward. Tomorrow, I was going to have to take matters into my own hands, and take my power back from this slimy player. I was going to do what I did best—defeat anyone who tried to get in my way.

TheRuiNar never backed down from a fight, and neither did Reyna Cheng.

FIFTEEN

If anyone asked me what I did the day of the finals, I'd answer, truthfully, that I didn't remember. The whole day passed by in bits and pieces of blurry memories. It had to be the least relaxing Sunday of my life. My classmates hosted a pre-finals pizza party, but I was feeling way too queasy to eat pizza. And I didn't want to risk any of them picking up on my nervousness and guessing the truth about why.

So instead, I found an empty classroom, closed the door, and blasted my favorite tunes for the whole afternoon before the tournament, trying to lose myself in my favorite music. If there were a tournament for singing K-pop off-key, I'd win it *easily*.

I was the most nervous I'd ever been in my whole life. Including the time Baba and I rode the tallest roller coaster at

Space World. Including the time I played in the Spring Dayhold Games, making my public debut in the amateur circuits as TheRuiNar.

As I headed up to my room later that afternoon, I walked with my head down and shoulders hunched over. The point was to make myself as inconspicuous as possible. Unfortunately, I wasn't inconspicuous enough, because a hand tapped my shoulder just as I'd passed the commons room.

"Hey." It was Nell, I discovered once I turned around. "Where were you all day? Henry and I were looking for you."

"Oh, nowhere. Just . . . had some family stuff to take care of," I lied quickly.

Nell squinted at me, as though he knew I was hiding something. I did my best to look as innocent as possible. Then he shrugged, and my insides sagged in relief. "You missed a fun pizza party! Mimi accidentally ordered anchovies instead of olives on her pizza, and man, you should've seen how she freaked out. Didn't know anyone could hate anchovies *that* much." Nell cracked up. I forced a laugh, but it wasn't convincing even to my own ears, and Nell gave me an odd look. "What's the matter? You tired?"

I bobbed my head up and down. "Yeah, that's right. I'm just feeling really tired today. Think I'll turn in early."

It wasn't a lie. The constant battle fatigue had worn me down to the bone. I was glad I was heading into the final round, because it was probably the last one I could handle before needing a nice long ice-cream-filled break.

Before Nell could say anything else, I said quickly, "Sorry. I'll see you." I turned away before I could see the disappointment on Nell's face. Hurrying down the hall, I half hoped he wouldn't call after me, and half hoped he would. He didn't, and for some dumb reason, I was kind of disappointed. I slipped into my room without attracting any further unwanted attention.

To keep myself calm in the final hour, I browsed the Dayhold shop. Shopping always soothed me. I spent my newly earned points on the next and final upgrade for my precious staff. The Ruyi Jingu Bang glowed in its final form, taller and more powerful than ever before.

I knew I was ready. Now the only preparation left was to eat a hearty pregame snack.

"No cinnamon rolls today," I told myself firmly. This round was way too important to screw up with a bad diet. Even if cinnamon rolls were the tastiest food known to man. If I lost this round due to a mid-match cinnamon sugar crash, I would never, ever forgive myself.

I did force myself to drink some coffee, even though it tasted as yucky as ever. The caffeine gave me a much-needed extra energy boost, along with my warm-up ritual of dancing to K-pop. Though tonight it was more like wiggling than dancing, because I needed to preserve all my physical strength for the final showdown.

I sent a text message to my parents, wishing Mama good luck on her surgery, which was scheduled for later this evening. She had to pull through. She just *had* to.

Then I rummaged through my closet for something to wear. Red was the color of fortune in Chinese tradition, so I grabbed my shining red gamer suit, which I'd saved for the final round. I didn't really believe in superstitions, but if red was a lucky color, maybe some of the luck would rub off on me today.

"Good evening, Dayholders!" chirped Commander Dayhold from the computer screen as I finished the final stretches of my warm-up. "It's a beautiful day outside. A high of seventy-two degrees and a low of sixty. Of course, it's always beautiful in Dayhold, but the nice weather in the real world sure makes it feel like something great will happen during today's finals, right?" He chuckled. "I'm sure you've heard me lecture you enough over the course of the tournament, but luckily for you finalists, that all comes to an end tonight. For the final round, you'll step onto the circular gaming pads next to your systems. The gaming pads will sync with your gamer suits and project you into the Dayhold stadium so you can greet your millions of adoring fans all from the comfort of your rooms. Then we'll return to Dayhold's most basic battle royale format for the round: destroy or be destroyed. The winner will be the last gamer standing. When we crown the winner, all the finalists will have a chance to introduce themselves and talk to their adoring audience. That's all I have for you, gamers. You have five minutes before we send you up to the fans. Good luck, and game on!"

"Game on," I said back, even though Commander Dayhold couldn't hear me. But my mind was fixated on what he'd said about speaking to the audience without our Codex helmets. Fear trembled through me, though it wasn't due to the usual anticipation of battle. I'd spent so long now hiding my identity. Hiding the fact that I was TheRuiNar. Now the jig was about to be up. And hiding my gaming identity all the time was getting exhausting.

Maybe it *was* about time the world saw TheRuiNar, saw *me,* just as I was.

I stood on top of the gaming pad, and my suit heated up as it calibrated to the technology. A clear glass tube rose up from the pad, going over my head and then sealing, leaving half a foot of air between the top of my helmet and the glass.

Even though I took long, careful breaths, I couldn't slow my rapid heartbeat. The silence in my tube made the beating sound that much louder in my own ears.

Thump-thump. Thump-thump. Thump-thump.

This was it. If I didn't win this tournament, everything was over for me. No $10,000 cash prize. No more Dayhold. My palms grew slick with sweat as I realized that this might be my last time wearing a gaming suit and stepping into a battle arena.

This might be my last chance to show the world my skills—to show the world who I was. Who I *really* was.

My fists clenched at my sides. As the countdown from ten began on the big screen, my eyes darted toward my posters of my favorite female gamers once again. The sight of them helped calm my heartbeat and breathing.

Nine...eight...seven...

What would LuckyJade847 and M00nshine do in my shoes?

Six...five...four...

I had a feeling I knew.

Three...two...one!

I shut my eyes, bracing myself for this moment. All around, I heard muffled shouts through my Codex's speakers that grew louder and louder. Cheering, I realized after a moment, as the noise reached a deafening level. That was the sound of cheering.

"Welcome, everyone," boomed Commander Dayhold's voice over a loudspeaker. "I present to you ... your finalists in the Junior Dayhold Tournament! Give them a big welcome!"

I opened my eyes, and my heart nearly stopped in my chest.

My projection stood on a raised platform in the middle of the stage in the Dayhold stadium. All around us, the cheers and screams reached a crescendo.

The other finalists stood on their own gaming pads, which were projected onto the four remaining platforms. In our suits and Codexes, nobody could see what we really looked like.

Stage lights beamed down on us from high above, and there were even brighter lights out in the audience. The resounding cheers and noise from the audience of thousands were like a wall of sound pressing in on the finalists from all sides.

Slowly, I spun in a circle, taking in the sights and sounds. This was surreal. It was like I was in a dream. I prayed that it would never end.

No matter what happened, whether I won or lost, I knew that this was a moment I would never, ever forget.

I could hardly believe I was here. In the legendary Dayhold stadium. Where the Dayhold World Cup was held. Where LuckyJade847 and M00nshine and all my idols played. I could hardly believe that these cheers were for *me* and the other finalists.

And I could hardly believe that we were about to battle in the final round of the Junior Dayhold Tournament in front of millions of viewers.

"Now the finalists will introduce themselves before playing their final round. Gamers, please state your username, where you're from, and a fun fact about yourself. First up, let's go with—Amefyst!"

The spotlights shifted until they were all directed onto Amefyst, who waved a hand through the air. "I'm Amefyst. I'm from Alaska. Um . . . I like Cheez-Its!" The audience broke out into wild applause. I guess they really liked Cheez-Its, too.

Next, the spotlights fell on DragOn. He puffed out his chest. "I'm DragOn. I'm from Kansas. I can lick my elbow." More applause followed these statements.

Then it was F3lx's turn. "F3lx. Michigan. Got a pet snake. Name's Biter." F3lx got the loudest cheers yet, although I swear I heard some booing mixed in there as well. Popular but controversial, as always.

Dustin955 went after. "I'm Dustin955. I'm from Texas. One time, I stuffed forty-six marshmallows into my mouth!"

Then it was my turn. The spotlights found their way to me, and I squinted under the sudden brightness and heat. My heart hammered so loudly, it threatened to leap straight out of my chest. My tongue was tied with panic. What was my name again?

"Um . . . I'm TheRuiNar," I said uncertainly.

"Louder!" cried someone in the audience. And unless I was mistaken, that was Nell's voice. Shielding my eyes against the harsh glare of the light, I found the speaker. It *was* Nell. He and Henry sat in one of the front rows, holding a huge, ridiculous-looking bedazzled sign that read: *GO, THERUINAR!* Though most of the audience was being projected into the stadium, my friends were there in person. And the sight of them raised my spirits.

Just like that, the nerves were gone. Or at least, if I was still nervous, it didn't matter. Seeing my friends in the front row, cheering me on, was a better energy booster than a whole pot of coffee.

"I'm TheRuiNar," I practically shouted. "I'm from New York." That earned quite a few shouts from the audience, since New York was a hot spot for the e-sport.

Once we finished our introductions, Commander Dayhold raised his hand for silence from the audience. They obeyed. An excited tension filled the stadium air. Now all there was left for me to do was win.

"Commencing the fourth and final round of the Junior Dayhold Tournament," boomed Commander Dayhold. "In three . . . two . . ."

SIXTEEN

"...one!"

The four other finalists and I logged in to the game and entered the virtual reality arena.

The roars of the audience vanished, the sudden lack of sound almost as deafening as the cheers had been.

I landed on a cloudy surface. It was harder to see here, due to the clouds obstructing my view. When I looked up, a huge glittering palace loomed before me, the colors red and gold, like a building straight out of ancient Chinese lore. I pulled my Ruyi Jingu Bang out of my messenger bag for the last time in this tournament.

Here, it no longer mattered who we were or where we came from. All that mattered was who would come out on top. Who would be crowned the champion of the Junior Dayhold

Tournament. And I was determined for that to be me. I'd come too far now to lose. Not with $10,000 and a whole shining future of playing Dayhold right at my fingertips.

A screeching noise sounded right beside me. Two realizations struck me simultaneously: One, that there was something buried in the cloud, and two, it had snuck up on me with frightening ease.

I didn't have time to think. Reflexively, I slashed out at my attacker with my staff. Another screech as the creature went flying back. In that moment, the clouds parted, and I saw it was a kappa, or water monkey. It leapt at me again, and this time, I gave it a solid enough thwack that it disintegrated on the spot.

"Plus seventy points," Codex said.

I panted, readjusting my gamer suit. I'd made a lot of noise taking down that creature, probably alerting any nearby enemies to my location. Plus, my vision was still obscured by clouds.

"Codex, clear my vision," I commanded. The helmet visor tried to defog, but it hardly had any effect on the visibility. Frustrated, I squinted my eyes to try to see a bit better and moved as cautiously as I could through my cloudy surroundings. All the while, I couldn't shake off the thought in the back of my mind that everyone out there was watching me. To them, I probably looked pretty foolish just standing here in the clouds doing nothing. That made me feel even worse.

The one time my friends were seeing me play as myself, and they got to witness me wandering around aimlessly in this cloudy battlefield like a headless chicken.

I still had my Codex to guide me, though. The pulsing red heat sources on the inside of my helmet told me exactly where the other players were located in relation to me. There wasn't a moment to waste, so I headed west toward the nearest red dot. Since my vision was so obscured, I was forced to rely on my other senses. Hearing. Smell. Touch.

That was how I heard DragOn before I saw him. A resounding *crack!* of a foot snapping a tree branch alerted me to his dangerously close presence. It was probably the only reason why he wasn't able to take me out successfully with a surprise attack.

I whirled around just in time to block the blade of DragOn's sword with the body of my staff, shoving him several feet back. A very narrow save.

TheRuiNar: Nice try.

DragOn: Ugh! A tree branch.

Without giving him a chance to gather himself, I went on the offensive, swinging my staff right at his neck. Drag0n ducked and then lunged at me, slicing through the air with his sword. Again, I brought up my Ruyi Jingu Bang to counter his attack. I tried to push him back once more, but he held firm against the force this time. And then I realized *I* was the one being pushed back. I dug my heels more firmly into the ground, but my arm muscles still trembled under the effort of shoving against Drag0n.

And slowly, I was losing ground. This was bad. Really bad.

Drag0n: Wow, you fight like a little girl. How the heck did you make it this far?

Seriously? We were in the middle of a sudden death match, and he had the breath to waste to ask questions like *that*? A mixture of annoyance and anger surged through me. The combination fueled my muscles with the strength to catch Drag0n in the stomach with a spinning kick.

He went flying backward, losing his grip on his sword. The weapon spun past me and then vanished into the clouds. Drag0n crashed into a pile of wood. Before he could get up or retrieve another weapon from his messenger bag, I was on him, with my foot catching him in the neck. I raised my Ruyi Jingu Bang, preparing to deliver the final blow.

TheRuiNar: Remember this, Drag0n: I made it this far because I came here with something to prove. And you're in my way. Bye-bye, Drag0n.

Drag0n: You won't win.

TheRuiNar: Really? Who's gonna stop me—you?

Drag0n: It's F3lx. I don't know how he's pulling it off, but he's cheating. You won't be able to win against him—unless you figure out how he's cheating and stop him.

With my staff mid-motion, I paused. Was Drag0n trying to throw me off? Why? He was good as eliminated already.

TheRuiNar: How's he cheating?

Drag0n: If I knew, I would've taken him out and exposed him already. But since you've got a real shot at winning, I'll say this much: If you can figure it out . . . if you can do that, you'll deserve to win. That's a big "if," though.

TheRuiNar: No "if." I will win, *period.*

And with that, I slammed down with my Ruyi Jingu Bang, hard. DragOn disappeared beneath my feet.

"Plus three hundred points," my Codex said.

I took a moment to catch my breath while mulling over DragOn's parting advice. Rumors were just rumors. And I knew exactly how little speculation meant in the world of e-sports—after all, everyone had just assumed that TheRuiNar was a male gamer simply because I was good.

But maybe these rumors did have some truth to them. The cheating would explain how F3lx always managed to come out on top even when it seemed like all the odds were stacked against him. Like in the semifinals, when those two gamers had cornered F3lx, they'd suddenly frozen and F3lx managed to come back from the damage.

Then there was that time when F3lx and I had nearly duked it out, but then *I'd* frozen as well.

A sudden thought jolted through me as I put two and two together. The freezing. That was it. *That* was how Felix was cheating—by somehow managing to glitch his opponents.

All this time, I'd thought that only an extremely talented gamer could fight like F3lx did. And it was true that he *was* talented. But what if it wasn't just F3lx's talent helping him best any opponent who stood in his path? What if he really was breaking the rules— sabotaging his opponents' ability to attack him, manipulating the virtual reality world itself?

And if my speculations were true—if F3lx was manipulating the Dayhold system to cheat—he'd easily be able to slip an untraceable email into my inbox.

There was only one way to find out the answers to all my questions. And it certainly wasn't being a sitting duck for the other gamers.

I checked my Codex, which revealed to me that all three remaining heat sources were clustered together, off to my right. I made a beeline in that direction. A few more creatures crossed my path—a hú li jīng and a tengu, a bird demon. I was able to fight them off easily.

"Plus fifty points," my Codex said. *"Plus seventy points."*

Finally, I emerged in a clearing where the clouds had dissipated. I was in an imperial garden, full of huge bonsai trees. There was a small pond with plenty of koi swimming around in the water, and a bridge constructed over it. The scene was so peaceful and serene, I almost forgot that I was in the fight of my life.

The shouts from the three gamers nearby brought me crashing back to reality. Amefyst, Dustin955, and F3lx were in a three-way battle, swords and shields clashing and clanging. Their movements were quick and fluid, each blow powerful and deadly. Even though they were my opponents, I couldn't help but admire how well they all fought.

But F3lx was really the one to watch. I hated to admit it, but in comparison to the other two gamers, there was a graceful, effortless art to F3lx's fighting. Each stroke he made with his spear seemed to be part of a dance.

It was clear to me, and probably to everyone else watching the scene. Amefyst and Dustin955 were doing well to keep up with feints and defensive maneuvers. At the end of the day, though, they didn't stand a chance.

I wasn't sure that I could bring F3lx down, but I had to try.

I charged toward them, just in time to watch Amefyst misstep and fumble his defense. I cringed, already knowing what was next. In one of the earlier rounds, a small mistake was still recoverable, but not in the finals. Here, a small mistake meant elimination.

F3lx's spear caught Amefyst right in the stomach area. Amefyst went down, and seconds later, he was gone.

Only three of us to fight it out.

Dustin955 was so focused on blocking F3lx's attacks, he didn't notice me sneaking up behind him. It was easy to hit him hard over the head with my Ruyi Jingu Bang. I almost felt bad when he disintegrated without even being able to turn around, not knowing who'd taken him out.

Almost.

"Plus three hundred points," my Codex said.

F3lx, whose sword had been inches away from taking out Dustin955, slowly lowered his weapon. He turned to face me. The Dayhold world seemed to disappear. It was just F3lx and me.

F3lx: And then there were two.

This was it. Everything I had been waiting for.

TheRuiNar: So I hear you're a cheater.

F3lx: So I hear you're a girl.

SEVENTEEN

I froze. Here, at last, I knew. Should've probably known all along, when I thought back.

My eyes narrowed. My fists clenched, already preparing for a fight. If F3lx dared to make a misogynistic comment, I was going to take him out right here and now. No mercy. No hesitation.

TheRuiNar: You're the one who threatened to dox me.

F3lx: Took you long enough to figure it out.

TheRuiNar: Why are you doing this, drawing out these threats? I don't get it.

F3lx: At first, I just wanted to dox you and get you out of this tournament. But now that we've come this far—and you still haven't dropped out—I'm going to defeat you here to prove to everyone that I'm clearly the superior player. Then, at the end, you'll be so humiliated, you won't be able to show your face in tournaments again.

TheRuiNar: Wow. You're sick. What have I ever done to you?

F3lx: You shouldn't have ever been in this tournament. Dayhold isn't meant for people like you.

TheRuiNar: I'll tell you what's really going on. You're threatened by me. You don't think you can defeat me, even though I'm a girl, so you have to use underhanded tactics to get me eliminated. Too bad for you that your threats didn't work.

F3lx: I'm not scared of you. Why would I be scared of a girl?

TheRuiNar: Why else would you go so far to get me eliminated? Do you hate me that much?

F3lx: You think I care enough to hate you? It doesn't matter to me if you identify as a guy, girl, nonbinary, whatever.

TheRuiNar: If you don't care, then what were those messages about?

F3lx: To win. No matter what. Which means I'm going to take you down. And after I reveal who you really are, you won't be able to show yourself around Dayhold circuits again.

We circled each other like hawks eyeing their prey. Emotions swirled around inside me. Fury. Shock. And the desire to win, at all costs.

F3lx no longer seemed like the impressive Dayholder to beat. Now that I'd realized the truth—that he was intimidated and scared of *me*—he seemed ... pathetic. I didn't need to be afraid of F3lx. Didn't need to feel threatened by a gamer who couldn't win without resorting to cheating and other underhanded tactics.

His motive wasn't just to get me out of the Junior Dayhold Tournament. It was to humiliate me, make my identity known in the hopes that I couldn't attend future tournaments. And he'd gone so far as to put his devious plan into action. At the realization, fury swept through me.

F3lx was the one going down. Not me. And I'd defeat him while playing by the rules.

TheRuiNar: There are rumors that you're cheating.

F3lx: Who said I'm cheating?

F3lx remained remarkably calm. His response was quick, smooth. Too smooth.

My gut told me that the rumors and Drag0n's words were true. F3lx was cheating. I only had a theory of how he might be doing it, but it was worth checking out. Every time the freezing had happened, it was when F3lx had been close enough to touch his opponent, so I'd stay out of range.

TheRuiNar: Everyone. Everyone's been saying you're cheating. We just haven't been able to figure out *how*.

F3lx: I'm done talking now, if that's all the same to you. This has been fun, but I have another tournament title to claim.

TheRuiNar: No, that title is *mine*.

I lunged forward, without giving F3lx the chance to launch the first attack, careful to not let him touch me. He sidestepped me easily, but I'd expected as much. I knew that he wasn't going to be an easy opponent to defeat.

But then again, that's what made Dayhold fun. The thrill of a high-stakes battle. Winning the tournament wouldn't be worth it if I didn't take down an opponent of F3lx's caliber, especially if he was cheating.

F3lx struck so fast with his sword that I almost didn't block the attack in time. Then he retracted his weapon, and I wasn't quick enough to pull back before he did. I pitched forward but caught myself with one arm on the ground and pushed off. I sent F3lx reeling back with a well-placed jab of the Ruyi Jingu Bang on his left shoulder. Before he could recover, I jumped to my feet. With all my might, I slammed my Ruyi Jingu Bang with pinpoint accuracy into the soft middle of his gamer suit. It made a cracking noise. Then, quickly, I leapt back, out of close combat range. I wasn't giving him *any* opportunity to get to me.

F3lx keeled over, motionless.

That last blow I'd dealt him should've been enough to eliminate any gamer from the tournament and make me the winner. But I had a feeling it wouldn't be enough to get F3lx out.

And sure enough, a moment later, my fears were confirmed. F3lx twitched and then got to his feet again, stretching out his limbs. You would've thought he'd just woken up from a nap.

TheRuiNar: H-how? How do you keep getting up?

F3lx: Because. I *have* to win.

I'd barely processed F3lx's response before, quick as lightning, he struck at me with his sword. I dove out of the way, but not before the blade stabbed me in my left shoulder. Pain sliced through me. Even through virtual reality, it stung a *lot*. My health bar went down by half. I seized a peach from the depths of my messenger bag and ate it in two bites, before racing back out to battle F3lx.

F3lx—Felix Matthews—the rich, successful, popular blond gamer, who had plenty of friends and fans. F3lx had everything. He thought he *had* to win, but that was because he didn't know what the view was like from down here. He didn't know what it was like to have nothing and have to prove everything.

Down here, where the guys constantly insulted the girls, forcing me to hide who I really was. Down here, where the only reason I'd been able to attend Dayhold Academy was because of the scholarship I'd earned through sheer determination.

The slow-burning rage that had built inside me over the years now blazed through my body. I was fueled by it. And I knew I couldn't lose.

TheRuiNar: No, *I'm* the one who has to win!

My mind went into a panicked overdrive, trying to do too many things at once: avoid F3lx's direct touch, figure out how he was cheating, and defeat him. In my distracted state, I clumsily raised my staff to shield myself from F3lx's next barrage of attacks but didn't do a good enough job. F3lx sent my Ruyi Jingu Bang flying out of my hands, far out of reach behind a cluster of bonsai trees. He moved in for the kill, but I kicked up dust into his helmet to slow him down. This wasn't time for pretty fighting. This was time for survival fighting.

F3lx staggered backward, wiping the dirt off his face. That was all the opening I needed to run toward my weapon. When I grabbed it, I hung back in the cover of the trees, watching F3lx struggle to regroup.

F3lx: You don't get points for hiding, coward! Get out here and face me. Promise I'll go easy on you.

I ignored his taunts. I needed time to think. It sounded impossible, but F3lx was disrupting the technology of Dayhold itself. He was also being sneaky enough about it, with his fast movement, that nobody except me and maybe Commander Dayhold could tell. The most perceptive audience members could probably see that

F3lx's touch was the cause of the freezing glitches, but I couldn't count on anyone else picking it up.

So how the heck was I supposed to defeat him while he had the upper hand?

F3lx's footsteps sounded near me. I quickly scurried away, running from tree to tree to keep cover.

F3lx: Come out, come out, wherever you are!

All our gamer suits were inspected before we were even allowed into the game world. F3lx couldn't have planted anything in his clothes. That meant whatever he was doing to manipulate the game, he was able to do within the game itself, without any outside supplies. He had to be disrupting the code of Dayhold. Would a teenager really be able to outwit state-of-the-art technology?

Now wasn't the time to question. Now was the time to *act*. If I wanted to gain the upper hand, I had to surprise attack him and defeat him once and for all. My gut told me that strategy was my best bet. Not that I really had a choice.

Now it was do or die. Either I'd shut down F3lx and his

cheating—or I'd lose everything trying. And I did *not* plan to lose.

Holding my breath and psyching myself up, I counted silently in my head.

Three... two...

...one!

I leapt out of the trees, successfully catching F3lx by surprise. But I'd slightly misjudged our positioning, and F3lx was able to dive out of the way just in time. He dropped his weapon—a spear—in the process. My determination fueling me, I kicked the weapon out of the way before he could reach for it. Each second of the final showdown was costly—and I didn't miss a beat of the rhythm to this strange, deadly dance.

I yanked a rope out of my messenger bag and tossed it around F3lx's body, pinning his arms to his sides. Swinging my weapon with all my might, I knocked the unarmed F3lx to the ground.

TheRuiNar: Gotcha!

F3lx: Get off me!

Grasping his helmet firmly, I raised my Ruyi Jingu Bang once more. The fully powered-up weapon was a sight to behold: It glowed a brilliant golden color, shimmering with power. One blast of the staff, and F3lx would be a goner.

TheRuiNar: A fitting ending for a cheater. So long, F3lx.

F3lx: Haven't you figured it out by now? You've lost no matter what. Who knows if your fans will support you when they know who you really are.

I swallowed the fear that spiked in me. The fear that maybe F3lx was right. But if I was certain about one thing, it was that he wasn't going to dox me. Not if I could help it.

TheRuiNar: We'll see about that.

And then I cracked down with my Ruyi Jingu Bang, hard. F3lx glowered at me until the moment his body had disintegrated.

"Plus three hundred points," Codex said. *"The Junior Dayhold Tournament has concluded."*

EIGHTEEN

Blinding lights and resounding cheers welcomed me back to the real world. As my eyes adjusted to the brightness of the lights, I cast a glance around the stadium. Once again, all the finalists were projected onto platforms on the stage, looking as exhausted and dazed as I felt. The audience whooped and cheered. Some people even began stamping their feet on the ground. Lights flashed as they waved their colorful glow sticks through the air.

"Esteemed attendees, your Junior Dayhold Tournament champion is..." Commander Dayhold drew out the announcement, speaking into a huge megaphone with the Fuzion logo on it. The crowd quieted. I leaned forward in anticipation, my heart hammering in my throat.

In this moment, with the eyes of all the fans on me, I knew I had to do it—to proudly show them who I really was. Now or never.

I leapt toward the commander. Before he could react, I stepped in front of him and turned my projection toward the crowd.

"What do you think you're doing?" Commander Dayhold roared.

"I'm sorry, but I haven't been totally honest with you all, so I just wanna clear the air and tell you something very important."

This was it. Do or die. In a matter of moments, everyone might laugh at me, or worse, boo me off the stage. The whole audience tensed, and even the commander froze, waiting for my next words.

Before I lost my nerve, I took off my VR helmet, with shaking hands.

"I'm . . . I'm actually Reyna Cheng!"

The audience fell silent for one eerie moment after my announcement. Even from here, I could see the shock on Nell's and Henry's faces. My heart was lodged somewhere in my throat. Were they all angry with me for leading them on? Were they going to crack jokes about girls in gaming?

Then: "WHAT?" shouted Amefyst, breaking the spell. "Wow! You look *nothing* like your avatar."

"You had me fooled. Like, *totally* fooled," said Dustin955.

"You're amazing!" DragOn chimed in.

The audience was in an uproar. I met my friends' eyes, but they still looked too stunned to react.

The shouts were deafening, but one rose out above the others.

"That's my daughter!"

My head snapped up. Frantically, I looked through the audience, trying to locate the source of the voice. And then there he was, standing a few rows above Henry and Nell.

Baba. Jumping up and down. Waving his arms.

Tears filled my eyes at the sight of my quiet, unassuming father, who was jumping up and shouting for me. I couldn't believe it. He'd come, after all. Even though he didn't like Dayhold. Even though he didn't approve of me being a gamer. He'd come to see me play. He'd come to cheer me on.

The sight of Baba filled me with enough strength to take down a whole army of Dayholders.

"Well, that was—that was quite unexpected, TheRuiNar!" Commander Dayhold's voice came over the loudspeaker again. I couldn't tell if he sounded pleased or angry. Most likely, he was just as thrown off as everyone else was. "Who could've seen that twist coming, right, folks? That's why we love the spirit of this game!"

Leave it to the commander to use my identity reveal as another marketing tactic for Dayhold. Oh well. He could do and say whatever he liked. My task here was done.

I felt lighter than I had in days, as though a huge weight had been lifted off my chest. Now Felix had nothing over me. The whole world now knew the truth behind TheRuiNar: that the amateur gamer who'd torched the competition in the Spring Dayhold Games, who'd made it to the final round of the Junior Dayhold Tournament ... was twelve-year-old Reyna Cheng. The youngest and only female Chinese American Junior Dayhold Tournament champion. And I'd revealed that knowledge on my *own* terms.

And nobody was angry or upset. They were *cheering* for me. For Reyna. Why had I been so scared to come forward as my true self again?

At last, I'd accomplished the one thing I'd wanted to do most: I'd proven to the world that girl gamers *did* belong in the world of Dayhold.

"I'm pleased to present to you the winner of this year's Junior Dayhold Tournament—TheRuiNar!" announced Commander Dayhold. "And the runner-up—F3lx!"

Amid the swell of cheers, I met F3lx's gaze across the stage. He'd taken off his Codex, too, his blond hair matted to his head. He glowered at me, as though he'd like nothing better than to chuck his helmet at me.

"She's not even that great a gamer!" shouted F3lx.

I couldn't be happy about winning. Not just yet. There was still one thing left to do.

"Says the cheater," I fired back.

"Cheater? What's the meaning of this?" Commander Dayhold demanded, looking between F3lx and me with shock.

There was no turning back, now that I'd accused F3lx in front of everyone. I had to stand firm for what I knew was right. "F3lx has been cheating. You can't crown him the runner-up!"

My proclamation was met with loud boos from the crowd.

"Sit down," someone yelled. "You're just salty that F3lx almost beat you!"

"Yeah, get out of here! Dayhold doesn't need whiny girls," jeered another onlooker.

I ignored the angry crowd with difficulty. There was no way I could let F3lx get away with this. But it wasn't like I had solid proof. If I didn't drop my accusation of F3lx cheating now, the audience was going to turn on me.

There was no use. F3lx was going to get away with everything he'd done to the other players.

Then I heard a voice rise above the others.

"Commander Dayhold, I've suspected F3lx of cheating for a while, too," said Amefyst, looking nervous but determined. His voice shook slightly at first but grew stronger as he continued speaking. "Many gamers have brought up concerns about him, and after playing with him and against him, I have a good idea of how he's doing it. I'd like to ask you to investigate the recordings for any signs of foul play."

"Me too," said Drag0n.

"And me," added Dustin955. "TheRuiNar and everyone else are right. Something about F3lx's play is off."

F3lx shot us all nasty glares, but none of the others seemed to pay him any mind. I flashed them a small, grateful smile.

Commander Dayhold made no move toward us, but he didn't dismiss us, either. He studied us, eyes narrowed. "We take cheating allegations very seriously, gamers. *Very* seriously."

I gulped.

Then, miraculously, a few other voices chimed in from the audience, clamoring for an investigation against F3lx. It seemed like it wasn't just the gamers who were suspicious of F3lx's easy victories. Some audience members thought it fishy, too. I mean, they'd been talking about it *forever*, but nobody had actually done anything about it, because nobody with authority would actually listen.

Until now. Until F3lx had gone too far, daring to cheat his way to the championship and even threatening to dox me. Commander Dayhold, Fuzion, and every other tournament organizer were forced to listen to us now.

When the shouts became too loud to ignore, Commander Dayhold stepped off his podium and walked toward the gamers. As he drew closer and closer to me, I realized just how tall he was. Over a video screen, it was hard to judge height. He had to be well over six feet tall.

Commander Dayhold raised his hand. "Silence!" he called, and after a moment, the noise of the crowd quieted down. He looked down his nose at us, and I suddenly felt very, very small in his presence. "I will look into this matter myself, rest assured, gamers. Dayhold values honesty and integrity above all else." When he said "honesty," his eyes flickered toward F3lx, who flushed and stared at his feet.

A muscle worked in the commander's jaw. I thought he was going to chastise us for daring to speak up, but miraculously, he closed his eyes and sighed. I guess he didn't want to mess around with this audience.

"I suppose a revision of my previous announcement is in order." Commander Dayhold turned back toward the restless audience and boomed out, "Given the new information that's come to light, F3lx, our runner-up, is to be placed under investigation for foul play."

His words were met with an uproar. Nothing like this had ever happened in Dayhold history.

"What? Under investigation?" F3lx yelled. Even from all the way over here, I could practically feel the anger rolling off him. "You can't make me a fool because of your little game, Dad!" With that threat, F3lx was gone.

Dad?

In confusion, I glanced up at Commander Dayhold. For just a moment, his poker face crumpled, and I saw the familiar weary face of an overworked father.

My confusion was matched by the audience members, who were gasping and loudly chattering about this unexpected piece of information.

"That kid's your *son*?" shouted someone. "Did anyone else know this?" Judging by the shocked murmurs, this was news to everyone.

Commander Dayhold was . . . F3lx's dad?

All the pieces clicked into place. Like how easily F3lx was able to slip in and out of the Dayhold system and deliver that threatening email to my inbox. How he'd been cheating all along. Of course F3lx would have extensive knowledge of the world—knowledge that even the most experienced players wouldn't be privy to— if the game's founder was his freaking dad.

"If the investigation does reveal foul play on F3lx's part, he'll of course be disqualified and lose all his gaming privileges. He has not—and will not—be extended special privileges because he's my son." Commander Dayhold fixed us with an intense glare, and it took all my strength not to squirm under his gaze. Then he smiled coldly. "Now let's hear it for our other tournament finalists—and our winner, TheRuiNar!"

The chanting of the audience grew louder and louder. A flush crept over my cheeks when I realized what they were saying.

"TheRuiNar! TheRuiNar! TheRuiNar!"

They were cheering my name. Cheering for *me*. They didn't hate me. They wanted me to be crowned the tournament champion.

I swallowed hard and bit the inside of my cheek, afraid that the pressure building behind my eyes was going to well into tears any moment now.

The audience was in an uproar. *"TheRuiNar! TheRuiNar! TheRuiNar!"* Their shouts reached a crescendo, deafening against my eardrums.

Commander Dayhold turned to me, his face holding no expression. He gave a slight, almost imperceptible nod. "We'll all look forward to following your career, gamer." Then he turned and walked back toward his podium.

A Dayhold official came up to me, smiling, and placed a holographic gold crown on my head. It was featherlight and shimmery, almost like a lenticular book cover. "Congratulations, champion."

"Th-thank you." Champion. It was going to take me a while to get used to being called that. I sure as heck didn't feel like a champion. I had a sneaking suspicion that the realization that I'd won—actually *won*—wouldn't set in for a while.

But the only congratulations I really wanted to hear was from people who weren't on the stage. My eyes scanned the crowd, and I grinned when I saw Henry and Nell jumping up and down, waving their sign and glow sticks through the air. I gave them a huge thumbs-up.

I looked for Baba, but he wasn't in the spot I'd last seen him. In fact, I couldn't find him anywhere in the crowd. My mood dipped. Had he left?

"Folks, you've been a wonderful audience!" Commander Dayhold shouted into the thunderous cheers of the crowd. "And now we'll conclude the tournament with one last word from our finalists. Let's have them introduce themselves officially!"

One by one, the finalists started forward and revealed their names. Amefyst was Patrick Greenberg. Drag0n was Jae-ha Lee. Dustin955 was Dustin Hall-Robinson.

I stepped forward under the bright spotlight and squinted out at the audience. Sweat beaded under my game suit, sliding down my back. The arena suddenly felt a million degrees hotter than before.

I straightened my back. My voice rang loud and clear through the auditorium. "I'm Reyna Cheng. My Chinese name is Rui Na. I'm from Brooklyn, and I'm your new Junior Dayhold Tournament champion!"

The applause that greeted my words was like a roar of thunder. And then the audience really did roar.

"Reyna Cheng! Reyna Cheng! Reyna Cheng! Reyna Cheng!"

That chanting was a sound that I would never, ever forget, for as long as I lived.

NINETEEN

My world had just changed. I don't mean in a visible way, like I'd stepped onto a whole different planet, or something. I got the strongest gut feeling that nothing would be the same from now on.

No longer was I an average twelve-year-old girl who just happened to really love Dayhold. I'd won the biggest amateur e-sports tournament in the world. And soon, if not now, every Dayhold fan would know my name: Reyna Cheng. Chinese American girl gamer.

It was as though I were in a dream. But even in my wildest dreams, I couldn't have imagined this moment. The dazzling white lights shone down upon me, and the thunderous cheers of the crowd pounded in my eardrums.

After the finalists said goodbye to the crowd, our projections disappeared, and then came that familiar jerk, leaving me in my room.

It was jarring to go from the intense atmosphere of that Dayhold-loving audience to the pressing silence of my dorm. My ears were ringing from the crowd's screams, and I was pretty sure they would never stop.

"I can't believe that just happened," I murmured.

Alone now, I realized that every muscle in my body was aching. It felt like my whole body had just gone through the wringer. I collapsed face-first onto my bed. If my parents were here, they'd yell at me for still wearing my gamer suit while lying on my bed. *You're getting the sheets all dirty!* I could hear them scolding.

At the thought of my parents, an ache of loneliness seared through my chest. Even the aches in my muscles couldn't compare to the pain I felt inside. I'd never been away from Mama and Baba for so long.

The first thing I did after I summoned the energy to move was check my phone. There were a ton of texts from my friends, both from Dayhold Academy and public school. I ignored them all to check the one unread message from Baba: *Mama is in surgery now. I will call you in a few hours.*

All the lingering excitement of winning evaporated, replaced by horrible dread.

I'd won my tournament. But what about my mother? Was her surgery going well?

I hardly had ten minutes to just lie on my bed, exhausted, before there was insistent knocking on my door. For a long moment, I considered just ignoring it and pretending I was asleep. I was in no mood for company. But then loud, familiar-sounding shouts came from the hallway.

"Reyna! C'mon, Reyna, we know you're in there!"

That was Henry's voice.

"OPEN UP, REYNA! IT'S US! IT'S YOUR BIGGEST FANS!"

And that was definitely Nell.

Smiling a bit despite myself, I summoned the energy to haul my aching body off my bed and open the door. Henry and Nell were waiting for me, wide-eyed and breathless, still holding their neon pink-and-green glow sticks. They gazed upon me like they'd never seen me before in my life. Like ... they were looking at someone they couldn't believe was real.

Trying not to squirm with discomfort, I gave them a meek smile. "What're you making those weird faces for? It's just me, guys." I might as well have been talking to the wall. Henry and Nell continued gawking at me.

I peered past my friends, at the commotion behind them. It looked like half the school had gathered in the hallway, curiously gazing on.

"Hey, that's her, isn't it?" I heard someone say.

"Yeah, holy smokes. That's the girl who won the tournament! TheRuiNar!"

Uh-oh. I had a feeling that if I didn't defuse the situation, things were going to escalate in moments. And I'd already spent way too much time in the limelight today, so the last thing I wanted was even more attention.

Quickly, I grabbed Henry's and Nell's arms and rushed them into my room before shutting the door. Then I turned to face my friends, feeling nervous. Both of them still had yet to say a word. I didn't blame them for not knowing what to say. I didn't even blame them if they decided they hated me. After all, I'd been hiding this huge secret from them for weeks, making up excuses and sometimes even straight-up lies. If I were Henry or Nell, I'd be *really* upset with me.

For a moment, there was only stunned silence. Then the both of them started talking at once.

"Reyna, what the heck was that?" shouted Henry. "You—you just—you showed up in the tournament!"

"Not just showed up, you *won* the tournament." Nell looked gobsmacked. "You're the Junior Dayhold Tournament champion! Do you realize that?"

"You didn't tell us you were in the tournament!"

"You totally acted like—"

"*All* this time—"

"Can't believe it—"

"*You're* TheRuiNar!"

I sat down on my bed and put up my hands. "Guys. Guys. Slow down, please! You're going too fast."

Henry and Nell exchanged a look. They plopped down next to me on my bed, both still gaping at me like they thought I might disappear at any moment.

"It's just . . . wow, Reyna," Henry finally said, sounding calmer than before, though still shell-shocked. "I can't believe this. I can't believe *you*. You and I—we've been friends since we started school. We even started playing Dayhold at the same time a few years ago. And now look at you. You're . . . I mean, you're basically about to turn pro."

I let out a short laugh, waving off his comment. Pro? The idea still seemed so impossible and far away that I didn't dare to think about it—at least, not just yet. "All I've done is win an amateur tournament. I have no idea if I have what it takes to be a pro Dayholder."

"Do you hear yourself?" Henry said incredulously. "'All I've done is win an amateur tournament.' At twelve years old! Do you know how many people in the world can say that? Just you, Reyna. *Just* you!"

"Yeah, I don't remember there ever being a younger champion in Dayhold's history," Nell said, eyes wide.

I squirmed under their awestruck gazes. "Can you guys stop looking at me like that? I'm really not all that. I'm just Reyna. The same Reyna you've always known. My grades in class aren't even that great!"

"No, you're Reyna *and* TheRuiNar," said Nell. He kept shaking his head, as though in a daze. "I can't believe it. I mean . . . TheRuiNar is my idol. My *hero*."

It struck me then that my friend thought of TheRuiNar, of me, the same way I thought of LuckyJade847 and M00nshine. Nell looked up to me, little old me. The idea seemed so impossible to wrap my head around.

"I started taking Dayhold seriously because I wanted to meet them—I mean, *you*—one day," continued Nell. He stared at me like he'd never seen me before in his life. "And all along, you've been right under my nose. I—I even told you *to your face* how much I love TheRuiNar—I mean, you!" His face turned a deep beet-red color, and he stared at his toes. "Gosh, you must've thought I was such a weirdo."

"I don't think you're a weirdo, Nell. Not at all," I said quietly. "And I'm sorry I couldn't tell you earlier that . . . that I'm TheRuiNar. I didn't mean to deceive you. I just—I wanted to protect myself, you know?"

"Yeah," Nell said, his voice sounding faraway. "Yeah, I get it."

"Guy gamers suck sometimes," Henry chimed in.

Oh, he didn't know the half of it. But at least he realized how much harder girl gamers had it.

"But . . . I mean . . . you couldn't have given me a hint?" Nell shot me a slightly affronted look. "I thought I was your friend."

"Same," said Henry. "How did I not know *all this* time?"

"Would either of you have believed me?" I sighed. "I wished I could have told you, but no offense, Nell, I haven't known you for that long, and, Henry, you're bad with secrets."

Both boys stared at me, and then slowly nodded.

"I'm not the best at keeping secrets," Henry admitted.

Nell let out a long, low whistle. "I just . . . wow. TheRuiNar. *You*, Reyna. I can't believe it."

I wouldn't believe it, either, if I were in Nell's shoes. I mean, I *was* me, and I still had a hard time believing that I'd won the Junior Dayhold Tournament, for real.

"I did not see this coming," Nell was still mumbling to himself. "Talk about top ten anime plot twists."

"If it makes you feel better, I didn't see this coming, either," Henry said.

I hung my head, my stomach turning. If my friends didn't forgive me for keeping such a huge secret from them, I didn't know *what* I'd do. "I totally get it if you guys are angry at me."

"Are you kidding me? Why would we be angry with you?" Henry asked.

"If I'd been in your shoes, Reyna, I wouldn't have said anything," Nell said.

"Really?"

Nell bobbed his head up and down. "Yeah, of course. It's obvious how a lot of guys say horrible things to girl gamers."

"I mean . . . we talked about the tournament and TheRuiNar so much, and I had to act oblivious the whole time, when all along I *was* TheRuiNar," I mumbled. I turned to Nell, bowing my head in guilt. "Especially you, Nell. You kept saying how you're TheRuiNar's number one fan, and I . . ."

Nell waved a hand airily. His dazed expression had cleared, and he wore a half smile on his face. He was almost back to being usual energetic Nell. "I'm not mad. Just . . . surprised, is all. Like, *really* surprised."

"Make that really, *really* surprised," Henry said with a nod. "But guys are the worst sometimes, speaking as a guy."

"You're telling me," I grumbled.

"Let me know if you ever need me to fight any of 'em. I'll be your own personal bodyguard." Nell rolled up his sleeves and flexed a nonexistent bicep.

Though the move was unimpressive, it made me laugh. "Um, I'm pretty sure I'd have to end up defending *you*." Now it was Henry's turn to snort.

Nell rolled his eyes and then flopped down onto my bed, staring up at the ceiling. "Wow. I thought you were really good when you played at Liam's birthday party, but I never expected *this*. Man, this is a lot to process. I just . . . I need a moment."

"I need several moments," said Henry, flopping back on the bedspread just like Nell.

I snorted. A laugh bubbled up inside me. I tried to shove it back down, because this was definitely *not* the moment for that. But somehow I couldn't stop. There was nothing funny about this moment, but still my laughter bubbled over. Soon I was collapsed face-first on my bed, giggling into my bedspread.

"What's wrong with her? Why's she laughing like that?" Henry asked Nell. "Was it something we said?"

"If you think about it, it *is* kinda funny how good Reyna got us," Nell said, snorting. "Like, we kept going on and on about TheRuiNar, and she was literally *right beside us* this whole time. Is there an award at Dayhold Academy for Most Oblivious Pair? 'Cause I think that's you and me, Henry."

"Speak for yourself," Henry snapped. "At least my grades are top-notch."

Hearing my friends' banter only made me laugh harder. I was in *stitches*. Nell laughed right along with me.

"I don't get you two," Henry sighed.

Finally, I came up for air and grinned at my two friends.

Both returned my grin. "So . . . we're cool, right?"

"More than cool," Nell reassured me, and Henry nodded. "Actually, this is the coolest thing that could've ever happened to us. My *friend* is . . . TheRuiNar!"

"Champion of the Junior Dayhold Tournament," Henry added. "Man, that's gonna look awesome on the résumé, Reyna."

"You do owe us some matches, though." Nell pointed at me. "And no matter what happens or how famous you get, you'll always have to tell people that I, Nell Kwon, am your biggest fan." He flashed me a huge smile, his cheeks turning slightly pink.

My cheeks heated a little, too. I returned his smile. "Deal."

"What about me?" Henry cut in, frowning. "Reyna, I was your friend first!"

"Yeah, but before, you were all, 'F3lx this, F3lx that,'" Nell said. "And look how he turned out. He almost cheated TheRui—I mean Reyna—out of her victory!"

Henry blushed and dropped his gaze to his toes. "Yeah, well . . . I didn't know he was cheating. I never would've complimented F3lx if I knew that he was playing dirty, Reyna," he said quietly.

"It's okay. F3lx was really sneaky about it, so nobody knew for sure until now. For what it's worth, though, he *is* a talented player," I said.

"Talent doesn't excuse what he did," Nell sniffed. "That goes completely against the spirit of the game. F3lx is trash."

"Yeah, forget that guy. From now on, you're the one I'm rooting for hardest, Reyna." Henry grinned at me.

Before I could reply, the holographic screen across from my bed zapped on. The blue lights flickered, and then Commander Dayhold's face filled the whole screen. Instead of his usual hundred-watt smile, he was wearing a stern expression on his face. "Reyna Cheng?"

I stood up so suddenly that blood shot to my head, making me dizzy. Henry and Nell followed suit. My heart pounded with sudden nerves. Commander Dayhold looked serious. Was I in trouble? "Y-yes?"

"I'd like to see you in my office right now, please." And without giving me a chance to respond, the commander's face disappeared, and my holographic screen winked into darkness again.

I glanced back at Henry and Nell, who stood there looking curious.

"What do you think he wants?" asked Henry.

"Maybe he's gonna praise you and give you your prize for winning, Reyna!" Nell suggested excitedly.

"Um...yeah...maybe." Somehow I doubted it, though. That hadn't been the look of a person who wanted to praise me.

My friends' smiles faded when they caught sight of my less-than-enthused expression.

"We'll be hanging out in the commons area, Reyna," said Henry, grabbing Nell's arm.

"What? Wait, no, I wanna stay here and wait for Reyna to come back from—"

Henry threw Nell a no-nonsense look, and I was grateful that my childhood friend could read the room. "Anyway, come find us later if you're back before lights-out."

It was already getting late, so somehow I doubted I'd be celebrating with them later, but I nodded.

"Oh, I just remembered—we ordered cake as soon as we got back from the tournament! It'll be here any moment. You'd better come sooner rather than later, Reyna, before I eat the whole thing," Nell threatened. With that, he and Henry scurried off.

I took a few moments to breathe deeply and gather myself, trying to believe that everything was okay. Then I left my room, going down the hall in the opposite direction of the commons room. The walk seemed to last forever, partly because I was dreading finding out what Commander Dayhold wanted and partly because I was dragging my feet to *make* it last forever. Luckily, the halls were at least empty, since it seemed like most people had returned to their dorms to celebrate the end of the tournament.

The irony didn't escape me that I, the tournament champion, was probably in the least celebratory mood of anyone at this school.

At long last, I reached the huge mahogany door of the commander's office. I walked inside to find Commander Dayhold sitting behind a huge black desk surrounded by stacks of paper. The walls were lined with bookshelves, with hundreds of thick books neatly color-coded on the shelves.

The commander's eyes narrowed when he looked at me. His arms were propping his chin up, long fingers intertwined. Someone—a blond-haired boy—was standing at the desk, too.

"Ah, good. You're both here now," said the commander.

The teenage boy turned toward me, a surly look on his face.

F3lx.

TWENTY

Okay, now I really had no clue what was going on. Did Commander Dayhold call us down to his office to punish us both at the same time?

"You're probably wondering why I called the both of you here," said the commander, as though he'd read my mind. "That certainly was the most . . . interesting end to an amateur tournament that I've seen in a long time, thanks to you both." He turned toward me, eyes narrowed.

I squirmed under the commander's penetrating gaze. Even though I hadn't technically broken any tournament rules, he sure had a way of making me feel guilty as though I had.

"It's not her fault, Dad," said Felix flatly. Surprised, I glanced at him, but he didn't look at me. There was something wrong about his voice. It was emotionless, as though he were just relaying factual information, like a robot. "You know it isn't. Reyna played to win, that's all."

"You don't have room to talk, Felix," snarled Commander Dayhold. "I had my engineers take a look at the tournament livestreams, and they discovered that you *had* been manipulating the gameplay."

Felix hung his head, staring at his feet. His frame appeared small and shriveled. Pretty much unrecognizable from the cocky guy in the tournament.

When Felix said nothing, Commander Dayhold continued in an accusatory voice, "You used a bug in the code to your advantage by freezing players so you could easily defeat them."

No reaction from Felix, other than the back of his neck flushing red. His silence was confirmation enough.

Even though Felix's cheating was despicable, and he'd threatened to dox me and had nearly cost *me* the championship, a tiny part of my brain couldn't help but be grudgingly impressed by the complexity of his scheme. He was a couple of years older than me, and he'd not only found a bug in the code that others hadn't, but he'd also used it to do his bidding. Felix was pretty intelligent, and he'd also had access to insider information that the rest of us didn't. Too bad he didn't use his resources for good instead of evil.

Commander Dayhold's nostrils flared as he glowered at Felix. Then he turned his gaze on me, and I flinched. "As for you, Reyna—"

"I'm sorry, but..." I interrupted in a squeaky voice. I hadn't finished speaking up for myself yet. "I...Commander, Felix didn't only cheat. He also anonymously threatened to dox me." I paused and glanced over at Felix, but he wasn't even looking at me. Maybe he couldn't bring himself to do it. He stared at the ground, the back of his neck slowly reddening. Cold sweat lined my palm. I was terrified, but I forced myself to keep talking. Someone had to speak up for the gamers of color, and especially the girls. "Girls get targeted in this game all the time. I don't want anything like this to happen to anyone ever again."

The commander's eyebrows rose, and the glare he gave his son could have wilted a whole garden. "Rest assured, Reyna, that the punishment will fit the crime. Dayhold will not tolerate cheating, doxing, or harassment toward any gamers—now or in the future. I plan to speak to the other tournament participants who were wrongfully eliminated due to my son's cheating. We'll set an apt example with Felix's punishment."

"What kind of punishment? Specifically," I pressed. Adults sometimes needed encouragement to follow through with their words. And I didn't intend to let Felix squeak by with a lax punishment just because Commander Dayhold was his father. He'd gotten away with far too much already. "Felix *threatened* me into revealing my identity, even when I wasn't ready yet. No one should be forced to reveal their identity without their consent. Otherwise, how can we even feel safe playing Dayhold?"

The commander's smile slipped as he turned his attention to his son and then back to me. His eyes were cold, and his mouth formed a harsh line. "I understand the gravity of my son's actions, Reyna. He'll be banned from all Dayhold tournaments for a year—at least. After that year, we'll reassess if Felix's behavior has changed enough to let him resume gameplay. And at the time of reassessment, we'll ask for your input, too, Reyna. If you're not comfortable with him ever returning to official Dayhold gameplay, then I'll be sure he's banned forever."

It was a harsh punishment, but I didn't feel that bad for Felix. After all, he'd cheated. He'd come after me. Unless he had a true change of heart, what was to stop him from causing more harm in the future? "Okay," I said with a nod at Commander Dayhold. "And you should rethink the part of the tournament where the finalists have to reveal their identities in the end. Some gamers might want to keep that info private."

"We'll tweak the rules on that moving forward," the commander reassured me.

Felix, shoulders hunched, stared pointedly at the stapler in the corner of the desk. If he had any objections to Commander Dayhold's words, he didn't voice them. Maybe he'd already accepted his fate.

"Son, I had some pros ask about you, too, but whether or not I'll be recommending you to any teams in the future remains to be seen. There's no rooms for cheaters or doxers in any Dayhold circuits."

Felix's shoulder twitched, but he said nothing. Suddenly, a tiny part of me felt bad for him even after everything he'd done to me. He'd grown up with a really harsh, strict father, who seemed more concerned about work than about his own son.

Commander Dayhold shook his head in disappointment. "What on earth were you thinking, Felix? Did you want to ruin your career before it started? Or did you want to destroy our family's reputation? Or was it both? Help me understand, because I've been trying, and I truly cannot."

"Yeah, Dad," spat Felix, his fists clenching up at his sides. "I proved just how easily gamers can con your system. Ever since Dayhold became the number one e-sport in the world, you've been absent. All you want to do is go on fancy business trips all across the world. You're obsessed with Dayhold. You don't care about anything else. You don't care about Mom, and you don't care about me!"

I stared at my toes, feeling uncomfortable; I was basically listening in on a private conversation. But strangely enough, a lot of Felix's words hit home. Commander Dayhold sounded like a distant father who was having trouble connecting with his child. Just like ... well ... Baba.

I would never agree with Felix's decisions to cheat or blackmail, but I could kind of understand the years of pain that had led up to it.

When Felix was finished with his outburst, the commander's face reddened like a beet. His hands clenched into fists and shook. I was afraid he was going to start yelling. But then he closed his eyes and took a deep breath. "I . . . I have been away a lot, son. For that, I apologize. I didn't realize that it bothered you that much."

"Why would it bother me that my own dad would rather pay attention to a *game* than spend time with his family?" Felix said bitterly.

Commander Dayhold opened his mouth to respond but seemed to think better of it. He shook his head and sighed. Then he glanced toward me. "Reyna, I didn't call you down here to chastise you or anything but to give you your check and discuss your professional career."

"P-professional career?"

Impossibly, Commander Dayhold's lips lifted into a small smile. "I've already had lots of agents and managers at pro e-sports teams call in asking about you."

My eyes popped wide open. I couldn't believe what I was hearing. "Wh-what?"

"If you ask me, and I do consider myself to be somewhat of a Dayhold expert"—here he winked—"there's a long, fruitful Dayhold career in your future."

A flush of pride crept up my cheeks. Hearing the Dayhold

founder himself praise me and tell me I had a career in e-sports had to be among the top five moments of my *life*. I was definitely tattooing this memory into my brain.

"And here is your check. I'll forward the emails I received from agents and managers to your email. You're free to go. You should head back to your room." When I just stood there, he gave me a strange look. "Unless . . . you have anything else you want to say?"

Felix's head hung lower. A tiny bit of guilt twinged in me at the sight, but Felix had brought this upon himself. It was time he faced the music. Maybe after this, he'd finally learn his lesson.

"No, thank you. See you around," I muttered as I left the room. Maybe we'd face off fair and square on the Dayhold battleground one day—where I'd still clobber him, of course. Otherwise, I was going to do my best to forget Felix entirely and move on.

Reyna might be more forgiving, but as TheRuiNar, I was ruthless.

As I left the office, Commander Dayhold called after me, reminding me of something that I'd almost forgotten—that my meet and greet with the Fuzion team would take place tomorrow. Felix eyed me with envy.

In all the excitement of everything that had transpired, I'd almost forgotten this extremely important detail. Tomorrow, I'd get to meet my Dayhold idols!

With a new spring in my step, I headed to the commons area. Just like they'd promised, Henry and Nell had ordered a giant chocolate ice cream cake, my favorite. They'd also invited Liam, Mimi, and Sanjeet, which meant that by extension, every single underclassman in our school came to the celebration.

The only people missing from the small party, who'd make this day the best in my life, were Baba and Mama. But they were on my mind the whole time as I worried over Mama's surgery.

"Why do you keep looking at the clock?" Henry asked me around a mouthful of cake. Then his eyes widened, as though he'd just remembered something important. "Oh. Your mom's surgery?"

I nodded. "It should be over in an hour."

He bit his lip, his eyebrows furrowing in concern. "I really hope it's going well."

"Me too." My stomach was knotted. It took all my strength just to focus on not puking out of nervousness.

"Hey, Reyna, what're you sulking in the corner for?" Before I could register what was happening, Mimi had grabbed my hand and pulled me away from Henry, over to the half-eaten cake. "You have to have another slice! Everyone is stuffed, and it's *your* cake!"

My classmates made me talk about myself and sign so many napkins that my voice was hoarse and I could hardly raise my arms by the end of it. Plus, I ate way too much cake, and now all I wanted to do was sleep for a long, long time. But there was one more thing I needed to do. I slipped out of the party by saying that I needed to make an important call—which was true.

I checked the clock and then dialed Baba's cell number on the phone. It rang once . . . twice . . . three times . . . and then, when my heart was sinking and I was imagining that the surgery had gone horribly wrong, a *click* sounded on the other end.

"Rui Na? I was just about to call you."

"Baba! How did Mama's surgery go?" I asked breathlessly. My heart thundered as I waited to hear my father's answer.

A noise came from the phone. It sounded like a mixture of choking and sobbing. For one brief, terrifying moment, I was convinced I knew what had happened—that Mama hadn't made it after all.

Then: "She did it, Rui Na. Your mother did great. She's sleeping now."

Tears of relief and happiness fell from my eyes. In that moment, knowing that Mama's surgery was successful was better than winning ten tournaments all at once.

I went to bed that evening and fell asleep almost before my head hit the pillow.

TWENTY-ONE

I slept for twelve straight hours hours and almost missed my noon appointment with the Fuzion team. Luckily, I'd set my alarm the day before and was jerked away from a deep, well-needed slumber by the sound of an upbeat BXS song.

Blinking the sleep out of my eyes, I checked my phone for the time. It was a few minutes past eleven, which meant I only had an hour to get ready before my ride to Fuzion headquarters would pull up outside the front entrance of school.

I groaned and rolled over, burying my face into my pillow. I felt like I'd barely gotten any rest. My body was still aching from the brutal beating it had taken over the course of the intense tournament. I wished the Fuzion team had waited just a couple more days for the meet-and-greet event, when I could actually look and feel like a regular human and not a zombie.

Oh well. Guess I just had to suck it up and make the most of it. There was no way I was missing out on this day. Dragging myself out of bed, I threw on one of my nicer blue T-shirts and paired it with black jeans. Within forty-five minutes—the exact length of my K-pop playlist—I'd brushed my teeth, detangled my hair of its most unruly knots, and headed out of the room.

According to the message I'd received from Commander Dayhold earlier that morning, I was supposed to go to the front of the school to catch my ride to Fuzion headquarters. Sure enough, a sleek, black, electric-powered car was waiting for me outside the school.

The driver, a middle-aged man who was bald except for brown sideburns, stepped out of the car. He looked vaguely familiar, but I couldn't figure out why. "Miss Reyna Cheng?"

"Um, yes," I said, blinking. I wasn't used to being referred to as "miss." Come to think of it, I couldn't remember ever having a chauffeur before (unless I counted Baba, who was kind of forced to drive me everywhere, since that's the point of fathers).

"I'm Carl Young. I'm a reserve player on the Fuzion team."

Oh. So *that's* why Carl looked familiar. I'd definitely seen him play for Fuzion at some point.

He held out his hand. I stared at it stupidly, until I realized I was supposed to shake it. "Congratulations on winning the Junior Dayhold Tournament."

"Th-thank you." Wow. Carl Young. A real-life e-sports player. And I was shaking hands with him. Yeah, forget hygiene, I was *never* washing this hand again.

Some students who were hanging around outside gasped and whispered to each other as the driver opened the door for me and I stepped inside. I felt like total royalty. It was different, but not in a bad way. I could definitely get used to the special treatment.

Leaving campus for the first time in several weeks felt weird and freeing. Fuzion headquarters was only a thirty-minute drive away, so soon enough, we were pulling into the parking lot.

The Fuzion building was decorated with the huge Fuzion logo, which was the word "Fuzion" in big red block letters with a cross made of two swords behind it. The sleek black skyscraper looked like it had been newly renovated, and I had to crane my neck to see all the way to the top.

"There are a hundred and fifty floors in this building," said Carl, with a chuckle.

"*What?*" I gasped. "But what . . . what about gravity?"

"Yeah, that was my reaction when I got recruited here a couple years ago, too."

As we headed inside the gravity-defying building, a gust of cold air greeted me, along with three people wearing the Fuzion team uniform. One of them, a super-familiar-looking young Asian woman with long black hair that swished when she walked, stepped forward and smiled at me.

I *knew* who she was. But in the heat of the moment, I was totally blanking on her name. Ugh. *Why are you like this, Reyna?*

I was still trying to figure out who the girl was when she said politely, "Reyna Cheng?"

"Y-yes."

"Nice to meet you. I'm Sylvia Lin, although I go by SylverMyst in Dayhold."

"Wow." Sylvia was one of the newest recruits, but I'd definitely seen her play before. If my memory was correct, Sylvia, like Jessica Yoon, had been one of the youngest professional e-sports recruits ever when Fuzion had signed her straight out of high school, at seventeen years old. "Hi. Um, you—you're amazing!" I blurted, and immediately wished a hole would open up in the floor and swallow me. *Way to play it cool.*

Sylvia didn't seem to mind that I was being totally uncool, though. Her smile widened. "Thank you. It's nice to meet a fellow Chinese American gamer." She winked.

A warmth flooded my body from head to toe. It was like we had an automatic connection that made me feel right at home. A shared experience. I felt a lot calmer with her here.

The other team members stepped forward and introduced themselves one at a time. I was too shy and starstruck to tell them that I actually already knew their names.

Marcus Fisher. Paul Matson. Kiana Lewis. Shohei Uchimura. And—

"Jessica Yoon," I gasped before LuckyJade847 could introduce herself.

"Looks like the kid's a fan," said Kiana, bumping her hip into Jessica's.

The Korean American gamer with a short black pixie cut grinned at me. "You've heard of me!"

"I've heard of all of you," I admitted. "I—I've been watching

Dayhold streams for so long. You guys are my heroes. Especially you, LuckyJade—I mean, Mrs. Yoon."

"Call me Jessica," she said. "And I saw how you wiped the floor with all your competitors during the tournament, Reyna. *I'm* a fan of *you*!"

I could have fainted right then and there.

The team members gave me a tour of the building, showing me around the offices where they livestreamed, the equipment room, and their break room. They even showed me the kitchen, which Jessica was proud to say was stocked with state-of-the-art cutlery and tons of snacks. The kitchen definitely seemed to be everyone's favorite spot. If I were on the Fuzion team, I'd never leave this place.

I tried my best to remember all the details of the headquarters layout, but I kept catching myself tuning out. It wasn't because I wasn't interested in the tour, but because I was a bit busy being awestruck over the fact that my favorite gamers—my heroes— were showing *me* around their headquarters.

This was definitely going down as one of the best days of my life.

After a while, Marcus, Paul, Kiana, and Shohei had to leave for some livestreams they'd scheduled for that afternoon. Sylvia and Jessica stayed behind, which I was secretly really happy about. The three of us went back to the kitchen, where they dumped a huge bag of Doritos (Sylvia's pick) and organic popcorn (Jessica's pick) into the community bowl for us to share.

"So, Reyna," said Sylvia, grabbing a fistful of popcorn, "what do you think of our headquarters?"

"Oh, this building is *amazing*. I can't believe there are a hundred and fifty floors! And meeting you guys is the coolest thing that's happened to me, ever," I gushed without thinking. I was doing that a lot today. *Keep it together, Reyna.* When the two women laughed, I blushed. "I mean . . . Fuzion is awesome. You guys are awesome. I can't believe I'm here right now." *And I can't believe how much I'm babbling.*

"We think *you're* awesome, Reyna," said Jessica. She pointed an index finger at me, and it was already orange from the Doritos. "Word's been making its way around the pro teams that you're the youngest champion of the Junior Dayhold Tournament *ever*. That's some record, you know."

I choked on my chip. Sylvia quickly handed me a glass of water, which I chugged down gratefully. "No way! The pros are talking about the tournament? A-about *me*?" I squeaked. That seemed impossible. I mean, I was just ... *me.*

"Yup. The professional teams and news outlets are all pretty tuned in to what's going on in the amateur circuit," explained Sylvia. "That's where we recruit new talent every year, after all."

"Some news outlets are already theorizing that you'll be one of the top draft picks for this season," Jessica said, and she sounded as proud as if it was her own accomplishment.

Top draft pick. I was really impressed with myself that I didn't faint at hearing that.

"Anyway, Sylvia and I wanted to talk to you in private," Jessica said. "You know, girl-to-girl."

Sylvia's expression turned serious. I stood up straighter, realizing that they were about to tell me something really important. "I'm sure you've already realized, but Dayhold isn't exactly an equal playing field for all genders and races."

I nodded. That was something I'd reckoned with since the moment I'd gotten into gaming. Guy gamers could be so nasty, and most of the people who played Dayhold were white, too.

"I wish I could say that it gets easier as a woman of color in the pros, but it really doesn't," Jessica sighed. "Many e-sports teams try to include diversity initiatives and sign on people of color early on in their careers, but unfortunately, most of these gestures are just . . . surface level." She said "surface level" the same way others might say "sewage rat." Jessica leaned in, her voice barely above a whisper now, like she was afraid we'd be overheard. "Sylvia and I worked extremely hard—*extra* hard—to earn our spots as regular players for Fuzion. Most women of color end up on the reserve teams."

My stomach dropped. I knew that being recruited as a pro gamer wouldn't make things any easier, but hearing this straight from two of the top female gamers in the world really drove the message home.

I had won the biggest amateur tournament, but that didn't change the fact that I was a girl. A Chinese American girl. And that meant facing extra barriers that most of the gamers, who were white men, would never have to consider. It would be like trying to play Dayhold with a toothpick while the other gamers wielded the most advanced weapons. Just the thought exhausted me.

"We're not telling this to discourage you," said Sylvia quickly, correctly interpreting my apprehensive expression. "We're telling you because we want you to prepare yourself as much as possible for the world of professional e-sports. That includes physically and mentally. To make it as a woman of color in this industry means working fifty times as hard as white male gamers to enjoy the same success they have. If you only remember one thing today, let it be that."

"Make that a hundred times," Jessica chimed in. She sighed and shook her head.

They were talking like I was basically already a shoo-in to be recruited. I didn't have the heart to tell my heroes that I didn't know if I could get past all the obstacles to make it onto a pro team, much less work *one hundred times* as hard as white male gamers, so I just nodded.

"You're young, so if you'd like, Sylvia and I would be glad to mentor you here and there," said Jessica, waving her hand airily.

If I'd *like*? My mind went dizzy with happiness. "I'd love that!"

"Great. We were hoping you'd say that. Here's my email." Sylvia jotted something down with a stylus on her handheld tablet, an xPad. My phone pinged a moment later, and a notification showed me I had a new message—from Sylvia—in my online profile.

Jessica quickly followed suit, sending her email to me. "If

you ever have any questions, just shoot us an email, okay?"

I nodded again. A small voice in my head screamed at me to stop nodding like an idiot and actually *say* something, but my tongue wouldn't work.

"Not much for words, are you?" Sylvia said with a little laugh.

I blushed. "Um," I finally said, "I . . . Th-thank you."

The two women looked at each other and burst out laughing. I didn't know why, but the sound put me at ease. After a moment, I joined in, too.

"Thank *you*, Reyna," said Jessica with a wink. "Seeing up-and-coming girl gamers of color is the best kind of inspiration for us old-timers."

"Yeah. I'm feeling pumped now! Let's do our best in the game tonight, Jess," said Sylvia. "We can't let the twelve-year-olds out-shine us."

After that, the Fuzion team had a meeting, so we parted ways. I made a mental note to send a message to thank Sylvia and Jessica as soon as I got back to my room.

Hearing the truth about pro e-sports' lack of diversity should've bummed me out, but I realized I wasn't discouraged at all. In fact, I felt the opposite.

I was fired up. I knew beyond a shadow of doubt that I was born to play Dayhold. Not just because I was good at the game, and not just because I loved it, but because there were lots of problems in the industry—and it was up to gamers like Jessica, Sylvia, and me to change them.

TWENTY-TWO

If I thought the tournament weeks moved quickly, the week after went by even faster. It was bittersweet, since it was the last week of summer camp at the academy. The summer camp students would have to pack up their belongings and leave for home by the end of the week. I was so not looking forward to going back to learning about fractions and photosynthesis in public school. Though I guess life wouldn't be so boring now that I had a public profile.

But before we officially moved out of the dorms, our professors threw us an end-of-camp celebration picnic that Friday. There was barbecue, s'mores, and even Chinese hotpot—a yummy dining tradition where you boil your own food in a giant pot that everyone shares. It was a beautiful, sunny day, and the weather was not too hot and not too cold. The perfect day for a send-off picnic.

The only thing I could've done without was all the *stares*—from classmates, from professors, from everyone. The weirdest part of being the tournament champion was dealing with all the extra attention. Every day, I was bombarded by new requests from reporters who wanted to interview me, which I ignored because my parents had told me to *always* be wary of strangers. I was too busy enjoying the last bit of summer to keep answering the same three questions from every reporter and their grandmother.

At school, my professors didn't treat me any differently, which was a bummer. Professor Lucien did take me aside after an Intermediate Strategy class to discuss how much he enjoyed watching my Ruyi Jingu Bang evolve throughout the tournament, though. A lot of students seemed to have a hard time believing that one of the youngest students at camp—and a girl, to boot—was capable of kicking their sorry butts at Dayhold.

But when I offered to battle them and demonstrate my skills, nobody seemed to want to take me up on that offer. Wimps.

At some point, when most of the picnic food had disappeared,

Henry and Nell wandered over to the crowd of students around me. I mouthed "Help me" to them, and they both looked at each other and nodded.

"Oh my gosh," shouted Henry, pointing toward the other end of the school, "is that the Fuzion team way over there?"

"Where?"

People stampeded away from us to catch a glimpse of the famous pro players, who definitely weren't actually here. The perfect diversion.

Laughing, Henry, Nell, and I quickly pulled away from the party before they could figure out they'd been had. We strolled through the secluded part of the park behind the school.

"Yo, Henry, can you believe we're right next to *the* rising star of Dayhold, the legend herself, the one and only . . . *TheRuiNar*?" Nell exclaimed, elbowing Henry in a playful manner.

"Gee, I hope we can get an autograph," Henry snickered.

I rolled my eyes but couldn't suppress a smile. "Oh, shut up, you two."

"You've gotten too famous for us, Reyna. We've barely been able to talk to you these days," Henry complained. "You're always swarmed by fans."

"Am not," I said, blushing.

"Pretty soon, you'll forget all about the little people," Nell sighed, putting a hand on his chest dramatically.

"Come on, you guys know that'll never happen," I said. "You were my first two friends—and fans. And I'm waiting for you both to join me, by the way. When we're old enough, we're *all* going to be drafted onto the Fuzion team. We'll make the best trio!"

"You're for sure going to be drafted one day," said Henry. His expression turned glum. "Me, though? I dunno. I've got a long way to go."

Nell turned pink and stared at his shoes. "Same here."

"Good thing we've got loads of time," I said. "But no matter what happens, we'll always be friends, okay? Pinkie promise?" I held out my little finger.

Henry grinned. "I'll hold you to that." He and Nell both hooked their pinkies on to mine.

"By the way, whenever you have a free moment from entertaining your swarms of fans," said Nell, "is it cool if we do an interview stream sometime before we leave camp?"

"Interview?" I blinked. I didn't expect an interview request from my own friends.

"Yeah. My older brother runs a Dayhold podcast, and he lets me host the episodes sometimes. I wanna interview you before, you know, you blow up." Nell blushed, looking self-conscious when I didn't say anything. "Only if you're okay with it, of course. You've probably got loads of interview requests."

"I doubt I'll blow up," I laughed. "Dayhold news moves so quickly, everyone will have forgotten me by this time next week." Henry and Nell exchanged dubious looks, which I pretended not to see. "But yeah, sounds good, Nell. Wanna do the interview right now? I'm kinda over the picnic already."

"Me too. Those hot dogs were so oily," Nell complained.

"The only thing I'm *not* gonna miss about this place is the school food," I agreed.

Together, the three of us headed back to the empty commons area. Nell and I managed about thirty minutes of interviewing before the horde of TheRuiNar fans found me again, and I was dragged into a Dayhold Pitch battle with Liam, Mimi, and Sanjeet against my will.

This was definitely going to take some getting used to.

I finally managed to escape from the gaggle of students by ducking into a bathroom and hiding in an empty stall. When the coast was clear, I didn't feel like going back to my room just yet, so I decided to wander the school.

Between the picnic and students packing up their belongings, the halls were emptier than I'd ever seen them. The camp had been fast-paced pretty much from the moment I arrived here, which meant I hadn't yet had a chance to really explore yet. Who knew if I'd get a chance to come back to Dayhold Academy for summer camp? Before I left, I wanted to make sure I'd seen every inch of this place.

I stopped in front of a hall with a banner hanging from the ceiling that read: DAYHOLD ACADEMY HALL OF FAME. Smiling portraits of gamers from the past ten years the school had been open were framed along the wall. I'd passed by this place plenty of times while rushing from class to class, and barely gave it a glance.

As I went from portrait to portrait, a few names jumped out at me.

Jessica Yoon—Class of 2064

Nina Valdez-Jones—Class of 2065

Jessica and Nina. Or, as I knew them, LuckyJade847 and M00nshine. From watching their interviews, I already knew both women had graduated from the academy. But seeing the proof before me made me feel one step closer to my idols. Years ago, they'd walked down these same exact halls, taken the same classes. And now they'd risen to the top of the pro world, to a place where so few gamers had gone, so high up that I didn't know if I could ever follow them there. Jessica and Nina were both playing in the Dayhold World Cup two weeks from today—I'd had it penciled into my calendar since forever.

I recognized the names and plaques of a few other well-known pros, but it seemed like most of the Dayhold Academy Hall of Famers had gone on to have minor careers or changed their careers entirely, giving up on their dreams. I hadn't heard of most of them.

"Guess that's life," I sighed. The world of e-sports, like all sports, was harsh. Only the lucky few would make it in the pro world.

TWENTY-THREE

That Sunday, I said goodbye to Nell, Henry, and the other friends I'd made at summer camp. Luckily, Henry and Nell didn't live far from me, but the other kids lived all over the country. I definitely got kinda teary, but we promised to all keep in touch and keep gaming together, so it wasn't all sad.

Mimi knocked on my door as I'd just finished up packing. She was wearing her black hair in two braided pigtails, and her two suitcases were behind her.

"Hey," I said. "Um, it was nice getting to know you this summer."

"You too. I just wanted to say that I'm rooting for you. You're, like, the best representation for all us girl gamers." Mimi smiled mischievously and leaned in. "And I wanted to tell you a secret. I'm

RHCP. I didn't tell anyone 'cause, you know, I wanted to keep a low profile and all."

"No way," I gasped. RHCP, the female gamer I'd knocked out in the second round of the tournament. As far as I knew, Mimi's username was Meemers—but clearly that was only her alt account that she used in class, the same way I did with ReyningChamp. I guess I wasn't the only one who'd been keeping secrets around here. "Hey, you were kind of mean to me in the game. You tried to stab me in the neck! Literally!"

"Yeah, well, I totally planned on winning. And next time we meet in battle, I *will* win." She pointed a finger at me. "You'd better not lose to anyone else before then, TheRuiNar."

I grinned. "You're on."

After Mimi's surprise visit, leaving campus was pretty uneventful. I boarded an electric bus with mostly gold-level students, which drove us out of campus and dropped us off in front of a huge, sprawling line of cars. I spotted my family's red beaten-up electric car quickly. Baba was waiting there for me—with Mama in the back seat.

"Baba! Mama!" I gave them both a hug and then turned toward my mother, who looked healthier than the last time I'd seen her. I climbed into the back seat next to her, and tears of relief sprang to my eyes. Boy, I was *really* teary today.

Mama's hands grasped mine. "Rui Na." Her voice was quiet but strong.

"Mama, how are you feeling?"

"Tired and sore. But I'm feeling better than I have in months."

"She's doing good," my father said gruffly.

"I heard you won the Junior Dayhold Tournament," my mother said, gazing at me with pride. "Your father told me all about it."

I smiled up at Baba through the rearview mirror, but his gaze was focused on the road.

"I tried to stay until the end of your tournament, but I had to leave to be there for your mother's surgery," my father explained. "I saw you win, though. I . . . You did great, Reyna."

Wow. I could count on one hand how many times Baba had ever complimented me so sincerely. Actually, I could count one *finger* . . . and this was it. This was the first and only time he'd *really* acknowledged my Dayhold accomplishments.

"I . . . Baba— Th . . . thank you." It seemed like I was having difficulty talking these days. Everything just felt so surreal, and I was afraid it would be taken from me at any moment. I was so

263

used to things going wrong, spiraling out of my control, that I couldn't believe all my hard work had paid off. That things were going *right*.

But this was real. The feeling of Mama's hands grasping mine was real. The pride on Baba's face was real. Mama's surgery had gone well for real, and I had won the Junior Dayhold Tournament for real.

I guess miracles can happen.

"There's something your father has to tell you," Mama said. From the back seat, she gave Baba the stink eye in the front mirror.

"Er . . . oh, yes." Baba sighed, like he was giving in to something inevitable. "Well, you see, back in my day, there was a popular battle royale game that was like Dayhold's predecessor."

"Battle Storm, right?" I'd heard vaguely about Battle Storm before, in school and from other Dayhold players. The game had been popular a bit before I was born, but then Dayhold took off and left Battle Storm in the dust. I had no clue where Baba was going by bringing up ancient history, though.

"Exactly. Battle Storm was eclipsed by the popularity of Dayhold, and it never was able to adapt to virtual reality gameplay the way Dayhold was. The failure of the game designers was really—"

"Get to the point," Mama interjected.

Baba coughed. "Right. The point is, Rui Na ..." My father let out a long, low sigh, the air hissing out of him as though he'd been holding it in for a while. "I'm about to tell you something I haven't talked about in many years, but when you learn the truth, I don't want you to think of me as a hypocrite." His eyes flickered toward me in the rearview mirror. I slowly nodded. "I've been a Dayhold engineer for years now, but before that ... I was a minor league pro. For Battle Storm."

My jaw dropped. "No way. You were a gamer?" I yelped. "You were a *pro*?" I couldn't believe it. My father, who'd always been against me playing Dayhold. My father, who *hated* the VR game. My father—a former pro e-sports player? I'd have an easier time believing Santa Claus was real.

"Your father wasn't just any player, either." Mama's expression took on a faraway look as she gazed out the car window, as though her thoughts were already a million miles away. There was a small, sad smile on her face. And another emotion that I rarely saw from Mama—pride. "He won an amateur Battle Storm tournament in high school, and became a top draft pick for professional Battle Storm teams. He was a rising star—just as you are now with Dayhold."

Wow. Baba had been . . . *cool.* More than cool.

"What happened?" I asked.

"Unfortunately, back then, there were very few gamers who . . . looked different," Baba said heavily. "Gamers who, like us, were Chinese gamers. My own teammates discriminated against me to the point where my performance tanked really badly. I was forced to drop to the reserve team. And when I couldn't produce results as a reserve player, either, my team dropped me. Said it wasn't anything personal, just budget cuts and whatnot." His voice grew quiet and miserable, and was laced with another emotion that I'd never heard in his voice before— pain. "Unable to sign with any other pro Battle Storm team, I finally had to quit Battle Storm altogether. I decided to get rid of all my equipment and trophies. I . . . I've been hiding this secret—this *shame*—for years, Reyna. I didn't want you to pity me, or feel ashamed of me."

My chest tightened up until I felt like I couldn't breathe. I imagined myself in my father's place. Making it so far, only to lose everything because of the fact that I was a person of color. If I was forced to quit Dayhold and lose the dream I'd worked so hard to finally achieve, I wouldn't know what to do. Jessica and Sylvia's advice rang in my ears again, and I had renewed appreciation for just what those women were up against in the pro circuits.

"Baba . . . I'd never, ever feel ashamed of you. I'm—I'm so sorry you didn't get to keep playing Battle Storm," I whispered.

"Don't be sorry. Being a pro just wasn't in the cards for me. I was very upset at first, but my life turned out well." In a slightly cheerier voice, Baba continued, "I'd always been good at math and science, so I went back to school to get a one-year master's in engineering. I enjoy being an engineer, and I raised a family—and now my daughter is the Junior Dayhold Tournament champion. My life turned out better than I could have imagined."

Despite the sadness I felt for Baba, a small smile rose to my face. I could get used to hearing my father compliment me.

"Your father and I have been very hard on you, Reyna." Mama stroked my hair, gazing at me with a strange mixture of sadness and pride. "We just wanted to protect you."

"Dayhold's more diverse than Battle Storm," I said, and then remembered what Sylvia and Jessica had told me about their experiences being women of color on the Fuzion team. "Although there's still a lot of issues."

"If you want to turn pro still, I won't stop you," Baba sighed.

I perked up. "Really? You mean it?"

"Of course I mean it. You won this tournament just to prove how serious you are. You remind me so much of my younger self, you know—stubborn and passionate, perhaps to a fault."

"Baba," I groaned.

"But at least you have the talent to back it up," my father said, with a small grin. "Rui Na, if being a pro Dayholder is your dream, then your mother and I will support you."

"We've always supported you," my mother reassured me. Reaching out a hand, she brushed a strand of hair out of my eyes. "We just . . . we wanted to protect you from facing the same barriers and crushing disappointment your father did. We're so proud of you."

We're so proud of you. Words I'd waited all twelve years of my life to hear from my parents. Words I hadn't expected to hear ever, after I'd decided to pursue Dayhold seriously.

"We're even thinking that, once your mother is feeling better, she can be your manager," Baba said.

My eyes snapped to Mama. She nodded and beamed. "Are—are you sure?"

"Of course. You'll have many interview requests and new tournaments to enter. You'll need help. And back when your father played Battle Storm professionally, I helped him out with manager tasks here and there, too. I have experience." Mama raised an eyebrow. "Or should I apply somewhere for the position?" she joked.

"No, you're hired," I said with a grin. Then, to my embarrassment, tears welled up in my eyes. I furiously blinked them back. I opened my mouth but found that I was so choked up that words wouldn't come out.

If my parents thought I was determined before, well, now I wanted to take the pro world by storm—for myself, and for the huge, shiny dream my father had had to let go.

That was a promise.

When we finally arrived at home, I handed my parents the envelope with my $10,000 check. They calculated how much would be put toward our bills and taxes, and it turned out there was still a whopping $1,500 left over for me to spend on whatever I wanted—though my parents insisted I put away most of it toward savings. Maybe I could finally get the latest gamer gloves.

I dumped all my luggage in my room. Even though I'd only been home for all of fifteen minutes, I was already missing camp. Missing my friends. Missing the tournament. I even missed Professor Kumar's Dayhold Geography course, but only just a little bit. I couldn't believe how fast the summer had gone by.

Sighing, I turned on my computer and found that there were fifty-six new messages waiting for me, most of them from agents and managers. Mama had already agreed to be my manager, but it was still exciting to get all this attention.

My eyes started glazing over as I actually read through the messages and realized they were saying a whole lot of nothing. Also, I was wary of trusting these strangers. What could any of them do for a twelve-year-old kid, anyway? I couldn't afford any of the training courses they were offering. Even though I planned to keep winning amateur tournaments, I couldn't turn pro until I officially graduated from high school. That was, like, a million years from now.

There was one message that stood out from the others. One from Jessica! My heart raced in excitement. I still couldn't believe that I'd actually *met* her the other day, and now we were talking with each other like friends.

Hey Reyna,

How's it going, champ? It was so great meeting you the other day! I just wanted to check in with ya.

We're still hearing about you around the news outlets, so I figure you're probably really busy being famous and all that. But when you have a second, there's this cool opportunity that Sylvia, Nina, and I want to nominate you for. Fuzion is starting an official mentorship program for young players of color, and this September will kick off the first year. Think of it as a trial year! The mentorship program will be held remotely and shouldn't affect your schoolwork. If you're interested, just shoot me a reply, and I'll pass along more official details!

Best,

Jessica

A mentorship program with the Fuzion team? And they wanted *me* to be part of it? I was so excited that my hands shook, and I couldn't type my response quick enough.

Hi Jessica,

Thanks so much for this message, and for showing me around the Fuzion headquarters the other day, too. Meeting you and the rest of the team was a dream come true. I still can't believe there are 150 floors there—and that you get to snack on Doritos whenever you want!

Yes, I am definitely interested in the Fuzion mentorship program. If it's remote, I can make it work, anytime, anywhere. Just let me know what you guys need from me.

P.S. Good luck in the World Cup next week. I'll be cheering on you, Nina, and Sylvia!

Best,

Reyna

I shut my computer off and had to take a moment just to process what was happening. With a new spring in my step, I headed into the living room. I found Baba kneeling in front of the TV, fiddling with my Dayhold Pitch setup. "Baba?"

He jerked and then looked up at me sheepishly, as though I'd caught him in the middle of doing something bad. "Rui Na! I was just, um—"

An idea struck me. "Hey, Baba, do you wanna play a round of Dayhold with me?"

My father blinked, and then a small, hesitant smile rose to his face. "I . . . I don't know, Rui Na. I haven't gamed in years. I doubt I'd be any good now."

"That's okay. I'll go easy on you." I threw Baba my extra Pitch controller, which he caught easily.

He laughed. "All right, then. Let's see the moves of the Junior Dayhold Tournament champion against a former Battle Storm pro."

I grabbed my controller and sat down next to Baba. The familiar Dayhold welcome screen lit up the TV, and I was home.

"Game on!"

START INTERVIEW TRANSCRIPT

NELL: Hey, folks! Thanks for tuning in to *Dayhold Unplugged*, your favorite podcast for all things Dayhold. This is Nell, filling in for your usual host, my big brother, Brent. I'm coming at you from Dayhold Academy summer camp—although by the time you hear this episode, camp will be over. We're fresh out of the Junior Dayhold Tournament, and I'm buzzing with excitement still. I don't know about you guys, but this was my most anticipated tournament of the year—aside from the World Cup! Today, I'm

here with this year's tournament champion, Reyna Cheng, otherwise known by her gamertag TheRuiNar. Reyna, why don't you
introduce yourself?

REYNA: Um ... hi. I'm Reyna. I'm twelve years old, and I'm from
Brooklyn.

[slightly awkward pause]

NELL: Give us more! Come on, don't be shy.

REYNA: I ... can lick my elbow?

NELL: That's awesome!

REYNA: It's probably my greatest talent.

NELL: *laughs* A lot of people would say you're pretty talented at
gaming, too.

REYNA: Aw, thanks. I've just worked really hard from a young age.

NELL: That's a good segue into something I'm sure our listeners
are curious about. How long have you been playing Dayhold?

REYNA: Hmm ... I started out playing Dayhold on PC when I was
eight years old. So, four years now?

NELL: Wow. That's a solid amount of time. No wonder you're so
good! Do you have any tips for those of us who want to be as good
as you one day?

REYNA: Practice, practice, practice. Practice as much as you can, and practice even when you don't feel like it. I've probably played for, like, five hours every day, an hour or two before school and then the rest after homework. That's been my schedule since I got serious about turning pro three years ago.

NELL: That's ... intense. I don't do anything for five hours a day, except sleep. During class.

REYNA: *laughs* No wonder you're so good at it.

NELL: Thanks! ... I think. Oh, shoot—I think I hear all of your fans coming down the hall. We'll have to wrap this up, like, super soon.

REYNA: Already? That's so quick!

NELL: You'd better get used to all the fans, because—HEY! Liam, get your friends outta here, we're in the middle of something important! I *hope* you guys know you are *interrupting* the greatest podcast episode in the history of—*static*—aaaaand we're back! Sorry for that slight interruption, folks. Reyna—back to you. It's your first post-championship interview, and you're already so good at this. You're a natural.

REYNA: No, I just enjoy making fun of you.

NELL: *loud sigh* Okay, we're getting off topic now—back to Dayhold! So tell us, Reyna, what's in your future now that you've already been crowned the Junior Dayhold Tournament champion? Winning that title pretty much means you're the top amateur player right now—and I mean, you're only twelve years old. That's how old *I* am. That's bananas!

REYNA: Aw, thanks. Dayhold is unpredictable, though, so things could change anytime. But I'm going to keep playing and keep getting better and better. I won't let anyone take the title from me while I can.

NELL: You'd better not.

REYNA: As for what's in store for me . . . well, I don't know. It's not like I can see into the future, otherwise I'd be winning lotteries left and right. I'm just a regular student for now, playing Dayhold in her free time. But I've got big dreams. Dreams that are so big, they scare me. And for now, I guess I'll just keep entering and winning as many tournaments as I can.

NELL: I really admire that about you, Reyna. How big your dreams are. A lot of people are too scared to even dream as big as you do, but you're fearless. It's inspiring.

REYNA: Of course I'm scared, too. But I'd feel way worse if I *didn't* go after my dreams. You know what I mean?

NELL: Yeah. I know exactly what you mean. So my last question is . . . do you think you'll turn pro one day?

REYNA: Nell, you already know the answer to that.

NELL: I do, but our listeners don't. So whaddya say? Is a pro Dayholder career in the cards for Reyna Cheng?

REYNA: Absolutely. I'm going to make it into the pros if it's the last thing I do. TheRuiNar's going to take the world by storm.

END INTERVIEW TRANSCRIPT

Acknowledgments

As a kid, my primary loves were reading, gaming, watching sports anime—and splurging all my allowance money at the Scholastic Book Fair. It's a dream come true to publish a book with Scholastic that combines those loves, with a spunky Chinese American gamer girl who competes at the highest level of junior e-sports and fearlessly goes after her dreams. I hope you enjoyed reading *Last Gamer Standing* as much as I loved writing it. I drafted this book during the summer of 2020 at a time when the pandemic was in full swing. Playing video games and writing Reyna's story were my main sources of joy, and I hope I managed to capture that joy with the finished copy. The book in your hands wouldn't exist without the hard work of many incredible people who have helped me along the way.

Thank you to my superhero agent, Penny Moore. This is the third middle grade novel with a fierce Chinese girl protagonist that you've helped me bring into the world, and far from the last. It's a privilege to get to work with you to tell these stories, books that I needed as a kid and that kids today have thanks to your championing them.

Thank you to my fantastic editor, Shelly Romero, for being such an enthusiastic champion for Reyna's hijinks throughout multiple drafts of this book. Your sharp editorial vision brought this gaming world and these characters to life, and I especially appreciate how careful you were with the representation in this book. Thank you for your tireless work in helping Reyna's story shine and showing girl gamers that they do belong in the gaming world. It's my utmost honor to get to work on a book with you, and I'm so excited to watch you continue taking the publishing industry by storm.

Thank you to my hardworking publishing team at Scholastic: Caroline Flanagan, the production editor; Stephanie Yang, the designer; Taylan Salvati, my publicist; Mariclaire Jastremsky, the fairs manager; Brittany Lowe in sales; Erin Berger, Julia Eisler, Lizette Serrano, Rachel Feld, Emily Heddleson, Danielle Yadao, and Sabrina Montenigro on the marketing team. Thank you so, so much for shaping this book into what it is today, and for being endlessly enthusiastic about *Last Gamer Standing*. Thank you so much to Kieron Scullington for your incredibly helpful sensitivity read. Without all of your support, I couldn't have typed "The End" on Reyna's story.

Thank you to my talented cover illustrator, Julia Shi. When I told my editor my cover thoughts, all I said was, "Make it anime," and you *really* delivered. As a huge geek who has always adored anime and games, *Last Gamer Standing* is truly the cover of my dreams, and it captures the vibe of the book perfectly. A million thank-yous, Julia; I am in such awe of your talent!

Thank you to the book bloggers, whether you've been with me since my debut or have discovered me with this book. I so appreciate how you continue to show authors so much support and enthusiasm for our books. A year of pandemic living meant a year of living on social media, and your online excitement for my books kept me going through the tough times of 2020 as I wrote and put the finishing touches on *Last Gamer Standing*. I can't thank you enough for all that you do for authors, for helping our books reach the readers who need them most. I am forever grateful to you all.

Last but certainly not least, to my family and friends: Thank you for being by my side through the many ups and downs of my publishing journey. Thank you to Amélie Wen Zhao and Becca Mix for reading very early drafts of *Last Gamer Standing*, and for keeping me grounded in this tumultuous industry. Thank you to Grace Li for not only reading this book but also offering your invaluable medical wisdom as the doctor-author Asian dream child that you are. Aly Eatherly, Francesca Flores, Andrea Tang, Lyla Lee, Britney Brouer, Elinam Agbo, Amparo Ortiz, Elora Cook, Rona Wang, Jamar Perry, Mingshu, Kianna Shore, and so many other wonderful writers and bookish folks—I'm so grateful to know you and to get to read your stories. Thank you to everyone who has read my books and supported me as I stubbornly embark on this wild journey to reach for the stars. Like Reyna Cheng, I'm just getting started. I can't wait to continue sharing my stories with you.

ABOUT THE AUTHOR

Katie Zhao is the author of the Dragon Warrior series. She grew up in Michigan, where there was little for her to do besides bury her nose in a good book or a writing journal. When she's not writing, Katie enjoys reading, singing, dancing (badly), and checking out Instagram-worthy restaurants. She now lives in Brooklyn, New York. You can visit her online at katiezhao.com.